STARTING OVER IN THE PAST

STARTING OVER IN THE PAST

ELLA RYDZEWSKI

WESTBOW
PRESS®
A DIVISION OF THOMAS NELSON
& ZONDERVAN

WestBow Press books may be ordered through booksellers or by contacting:

WestBow Press
A Division of Thomas Nelson & Zondervan
1663 Liberty Drive
Bloomington, IN 47403
www.westbowpress.com
1 (866) 928-1240

ISBN: 978-1-5127-3042-5 (sc)
ISBN: 978-1-5127-3043-2 (hc)
ISBN: 978-1-5127-3041-8 (e)

Library of Congress Control Number: 2016902169

Print information available on the last page.

WestBow Press rev. date: 3/31/2016

Author's Note

I have wanted for some time to write a novel for older women (forty and up), since there seems to be a dearth of such books, as if only the young experience mystery and romance. Midlife also brings numerous changes that enrich storytelling. Catharine gives up an impressive career, confronts intellectual and spiritual challenges, cares for an elderly mother, uncovers secrets about her deceased husband, and starts new relationships. The story occurs in a familiar place, with pleasant memories from my own past.

In the 1970s I lived in Juniata County, Pennsylvania. I discovered after moving there—for my husband's work—that this idyllic countryside was part of my heritage, so I have set Catharine's story in this very real place.

However, you will not find Midland Bible College in Juniata County, although it would be an ideal setting for any college. Midland Bible College represents every small religious institution of higher learning in North America and around the world. There people seek to instill into their graduates a love for God and their fellow human beings. Secular society may not understand their traditions, faith doctrines, and high moral standards, but they turn out citizens who enhance their communities and call us to a better life.

Such schools aren't without their struggles to remain relevant yet faithful, and their graduates carry on the challenge throughout their careers, especially in the sciences.

This is primarily a story of the people living that challenge in the rural beauty of Juniata County.

This book is dedicated to my long-time friend, Chizuko. The experience of Kenji, a student from Japan, and his arrival in Pennsylvania are partially based on her story.

I acknowledge her for her inspiration, and the many friends, including my husband, who have encouraged me.

CHAPTER 1

Washington, DC
2005

Catharine's first mistake was having her husband cremated, but she wouldn't realize it until much later. She agreed to the cremation to please his two sisters, Akiko and Hana, in accordance with their family tradition.

The unexpected passing of her husband, Kenji Yamashiro, had happened on a cold January morning during his regular run near their suburban town house.

The urgent ringing of the doorbell had awakened her. Startled, Catharine sat up. The sunlight coming through the bedroom blinds told her it was late. The green numerals on the clock showed 8:00 a.m. Then she heard the doorbell again.

"Kenji must have stopped to have coffee with Victor Hammond and locked himself out, Chiro," she said to the smoke-colored cat beside her. Throwing on a terry cloth robe, she ran to the door and opened it to a blast of frigid air. Two police officers stood in the doorway.

"Mrs. Yamashiro?"

"Yes."

"I'm sorry," said the tallest one, looking away. "It's your husband. We think he had a heart attack while jogging up a hill."

Catharine's heart jumped in her chest. "Where is he?"

"An ambulance came. The paramedics did what they could, but it was too late. I'm sorry, ma'am. We'll take you to the hospital."

Catharine's knees buckled.

The other man jumped to her side to keep her from falling.

◈

Catharine barely remembered the days after Kenji died. His sisters flew in from Tokyo and arranged the cremation and memorial service, while Catharine moved in an eerie unreality. Their son, Matthew, came from California. Her numbness enabled her to get through the Friday memorial service.

After everyone left on Sunday, the empty town house awaited her in deathly silence. It crept into her body, manifesting itself in wave after wave of panic. The waves flattened into continual anxiety, followed by shaking sobs. The next day took her to work, moving her, robot-like, into the car, to the seminary, and into class before students she didn't see, speaking words she didn't hear.

◈

A week later, on Sunday afternoon, Catharine wasn't dressed to see anyone; she wore a long, yellow silk robe over her nightclothes. She sat on her ginger-colored couch in a daze, wishing Kenji would pop out of the next room and awaken her from this nightmare. Stroking Chiro's soft, fluffed coat, she went back to nine days ago when the three of them had last gathered for dinner.

What is time, she contemplated, *that it has the power to change life so drastically? Why can't it be stopped, turned back, or moved slower or faster? What kind of a monster is it that no one can control?*

In the midst of her grieving, the doorbell rang, reminding her of the day the police came. Would she ever be able to hear the doorbell again without feeling panic? She didn't want to answer the doorbell, but she did.

"Marti," she said. "Come in."

Marti Gaston was her husband's assistant at the Physics Institute. He was a slim, well-groomed man in his late twenties; he was a bit stoop shouldered from bending over lab work and a computer keyboard most of his days. Silky, white-blond hair, a rosy complexion, and pale-blue eyes contrasted with his dark-rimmed glasses. At first she thought he had come to support and console her.

"I'm sorry to intrude, Catharine. I know it's Sunday, but I thought you would be home today. Our director, Dr. Kushner, asked me to come by and retrieve Kenji's work-related papers for the institute."

"So soon?" Catharine felt angry at the request. He must have noticed the anger in her tone because he stepped back.

His expression softened. "I know this is hard for you. But he worked at home a lot, and the institute needs all his research files. I want to check the PC too, but he probably copied work studies to his office computer."

"Do you have anything in writing authorizing you to do this?"

"No, but I will ask you to sign a paper saying we retrieved his files from you. It's institutional policy."

She thought Marti lacked his usual friendly demeanor; he seemed aloof. *I guess like a lot of people, he doesn't know what to say under these circumstances.*

"Follow me," she said and led him to Kenji's office. "I'm not sure what you have in mind. These two file cabinets hold his work papers, and I'll start the computer when you're ready. Call me when you want to look at the electronic files."

She didn't want to leave Marti alone, but she went back to the living room and pretended to be reading a magazine. She felt violated by the presence of the institute in their home.

Marti called from the study thirty minutes later. "I'm ready for the computer."

It didn't take long to find the files, and she stood by as Marti flew through them. She wondered how he could go so fast, unless he had something specific in mind. He ignored Chiro, who sprang up on the desk to oversee the operation.

Catharine signed the form, and Marti started toward the door with a bulging briefcase. Suddenly he turned back and faced her. "When you've had a chance to recover, I'll tell you about Kenji's research. He had been working on something Kushner wants to get his hands on. Please keep it confidential that I shared this."

"Of course," she said, surprised. "Kenji didn't talk much about his work. Keep in touch."

"Thank you, Catharine." He gave her a hug, and she saw tears in his eyes.

He left, and Chiro followed Catharine into the bedroom. She went to the closet and from behind some folded T-shirts took down a black Japanese-teak box Kenji's sister, Hana, had given to her. Inside was a sealed, letter-sized envelope.

Two months ago, Kenji had asked her to keep it safe and directed her, "Should anything happen to me, please don't give this to anyone but keep it in a safe place. It has something to do with politics at the institute. I want to hold it for a couple of years until some changes happen, and then you or I will give it to the man on this attached card." She shivered, thinking about her husband's ominous instructions and how they might relate to Marti's comments about the institute's director.

The name on the card and envelope was Miles Pollack, Esq.

CHAPTER 2

Pennsylvania
Two Years Later

At eleven o'clock on a May morning, Catharine waited in the reception room of Midland Bible College's president, George Kenny. She wore her favorite periwinkle-blue wrap dress and had swept her long, honey-blonde hair into a high twist. The door opened, and a man in his fifties, impeccably dressed in a gray suit, stepped out. "Dr. Yamashiro?" He said her name with raised eyebrows.

"Yes," said Catharine, rising from her chair. She surmised that she didn't look as he'd expected.

He gave her a firm handshake. "Glad to meet you. I'm Dr. Kenny." He showed her to a comfortable leather chair in his office. "You have a Japanese name."

"Yes, my husband was from Japan. Unfortunately, he died more than two years ago."

"I'm sorry. It must have been difficult for you."

"Yes, it was."

"HRS has given me your file." Dr. Kenny looked down at a folder on his desk and shuffled some papers. "So you're an alumna.

Catharine Weaver. I see you graduated with degrees in religion and English.

"Yes, I met my husband in English class, and later we took physics together. I am still interested in physics as it relates to the transcendent in theology," she said, rambling to assuage her nervousness. "I'm planning to write a book on faith and science for conservative religious thinkers." *We hoped to write it together, and I haven't worked on it in more than two years.*

"Wonderful. It looks like you have an array of published articles and books, and you coauthored an Old Testament textbook. There's even a science fiction piece. You have good references, and they all agree you think outside the box."

Catharine cringed at the cliché.

"The position available is teaching first-year Hebrew and Bible history classes," said Dr. Kenny. "I see you have a graduate degree from Fuller Seminary, and you've been teaching Hebrew and Greek at a Methodist seminary, where you got a PhD." He looked directly at her. "With your scholastic background, my question is, what brings you to a small college? I will bet you are coming back home."

Dr. Kenny's piercing gaze made Catharine uncomfortable. She looked above his balding head and then to his blue-striped tie. She clasped her hands together while he sat back in his chair, his fingertips touching like a steeple.

"I grew up in Juniata County, and my elderly mother still lives near Richfield, off Route Thirty-Five in the family farmhouse. She needs my help at this stage of her life."

"Oh, what's her name?"

"Elizabeth Brubaker Weaver. My father was Samuel Weaver, but he has been gone for several years." She waited for some name recognition from Dr. Kenny, but he didn't show any. She then said she had a son, Matthew, who graduated from medical school in California. "He has a family medicine practice in a low-income section of Los Angeles." Matt and his wife were expecting their first child. *I don't want to tell Dr. Kenny about the baby. I'm not ready to admit I'm almost a grandmother.*

"Good for him. You must be proud of him."

The interview continued for what seemed to be hours, though it couldn't have been more than forty-five minutes. Dr. Kenny explained the theology program, the college, its mission, the number of students, and related topics.

"Tell me what you like about this area. I'm sure you have some wonderful memories."

For the first time she felt excited about returning to Juniata County. Her voice became animated as, forgetting herself, her enthusiasm took over. "I love walking in the woods, bird watching, and having pets. I look forward to raising a few chickens and planting a garden." *Such favorite things could lift me out of my mild depression*, she thought.

"I think we have a place for you here. I'm glad to see you have stepped outside your church to get a wide religious experience. It will fit well with the history course and diverse denominations in the class.

"Take some time to think about what we've discussed and call me in the next few days. Then I can take your appointment before the college board. You could commute to Richfield, but it might be difficult in the winter, considering last year's horrendous snowstorms. I would consider renting something close to the campus for the winter."

He rose from his burgundy leather chair. They shook hands, and he opened the door for her.

Catharine danced down the ancient steps of the administration building under the azure sky and warm sun. Yellow daffodils framed an expansive spring green lawn, and the light sweetness of flowering trees wafted through the air. She walked rapidly to the parking lot, so distracted she couldn't remember where she'd parked her Camry. She looked for the telltale spoiler on the back but didn't see it. She wandered among the vehicles. Her car seemed to be hiding in a moderately empty parking lot.

Suddenly a male voice called from behind her, "Can I help you?"

She turned around, and a medium-tall man in a tan business suit stood there, smiling. An angular face with a slightly prominent nose and black curly hair, tinged with gray, triggered memories.

"Aaron Zadlo, is that you?"

He looked puzzled for an instant, then with a wide smile said, "Cat? Catharine Weaver Yamashiro? Whatever brought you back to the old school?"

"I haven't made it final yet, but I may be teaching here. What about you?"

"That would be great. I've been teaching here for five years in the Science Department."

"Wonderful. How's Mary?"

He stopped smiling. "Mary and I have been divorced more than ten years." Then, in a happier tone, he said, "But we have two sons and a granddaughter."

"And I have one son in California," Catharine said.

"I know. I read about Kenji in the alumni newsletter. I am so sorry," Aaron said, closing his eyes for a second. "He was a good friend."

Catharine nodded and shook off the shadowy reminder.

She noted his attractive smile as he said, "I remember having dinner at your apartment in Pasadena when Kenji wore a long ponytail and horn-rimmed glasses. He looked the part of the nerdy physics student."

"And I wore miniskirts. We were so young then."

She glanced around the parking lot with a growing fear that her car had been stolen. "I'm looking for my car."

"What does it look like?"

"A medium-blue 2005 Camry with a spoiler on the back. I just don't see it."

"Oh, then you didn't fly here?"

"Of course I … I did." She felt her lips freeze on the last word, and she closed her eyes in embarrassment. "Oh no," she groaned. "I have a rental car, a silver Impala."

"Like the one over there?" He laughed and pointed to a nondescript vehicle to the right.

"I am embarrassed," she said. "I guess I got so excited about the interview and the possibility of moving that I got distracted."

"It happens to all of us."

Not as much as it happens to me.

"I've got to call my mother and let her know I was accepted for the position."

"Oh, does she still live in the lovely old farmhouse going back generations in your family?"

"She certainly does. I'll be living there with her."

"Hey, keep in touch about your plans. I'll be glad to help with the move."

Aaron dug into the pocket of his shirt and drew out a business card.

"Give me a call, or I'll call you."

Catharine took the card, shoved it into her purse, and fumbled around until she found one of her own and handed it to him."

"Okay, I'll be in touch," said Aaron. "Or give me a call when you have a moving date." They shook hands, and he strolled in the direction of the administration building. She opened up her cell phone, put it to her ear, and paused. She watched Aaron move away, a slender, tall man—maybe six foot. As he approached the first step, he turned and waved.

She punched in a number. The phone rang several times before her mother answered.

"Mama, I've got some good news for you. I was accepted for the job here at the college."

"Is that so? When did you find out?"

"Just now. Remember I had the appointment today."

"You're right. I don't remember things so good anymore. But please don't give up your job. I'm doin' all right." Her mother didn't sound as happy as Catharine had expected.

Catharine felt disappointment, even rejection of her "sacrifice." Tears trembled at the corners of her eyes.

"Look, Mama, we talked about this. I don't have a lot of time, but I'll drive up to see you. I'll be there in about forty minutes."

CHAPTER 3

Catharine ran to her car and grabbed the door, forgetting to unlock it first; she rooted through her purse for the keys and found them at the bottom.

Flying down the college road over the speed limit, she went right. *Or should I go left?* After several unfamiliar miles, a sign showed 35 South. *Turn around. Relax.* Passing the college again on the other side of the road, she saw a sign reading Route 35 North.

The Impala sped across the verdant countryside and between hills the locals called "mountains." The winding road climbed and went down again through a series of small towns and farms. She passed silos, rusty-roofed barns, and old-but-tidy homes. Near Richfield, she saw the Mennonite Historical Center, where her family's records went back to Lancaster and Switzerland.

Catharine searched the horizon until she glimpsed a two-story, boxlike stone farmhouse. A shiny, steep-pitched metal roof now replaced the rusted one of her childhood. She turned left on the long road leading up to Jacob's Farm, named after her grandfather.

The car bumped over the road. It had been paved once but not cared for, and the worn, gray-colored asphalt lay broken as if it had experienced a mild earthquake. A ragged green lawn in need of mowing surrounded the house. She parked in front of the porch built across the face of the house. There, sitting in her rocking chair, was her mother. Alighting from the car, Catharine ran up the gray concrete steps and hugged her.

"It's wonderful to see you, Mama. I have only a few minutes to visit, as I must get to the airport at Harrisburg, but I wanted to talk to you. How are you doing?"

"The same as yesterday when I talked to you on the phone," she said. She hugged her daughter and placed a kiss, which felt like a feather, on her cheek.

Using a wooden cane, the elderly woman stood up slowly. She wore a frumpy pink housedress over her paunchy midriff and rolled-up-to the-knee support hose on still-shapely legs. Dull, brownish-red, fine hair lay in thin waves over pink scalp and no longer covered her protruding ears. Her face, wrinkled less than expected, showed an aged beauty.

"I guess you're not ready for me to move in, from what you said on the phone." Catharine regretted her words as soon as they came out. Her tone sounded defensive.

"Of course I am," she said. "Would I deny my own daughter to come home?" She sounded incredulous.

"But you seemed disappointed."

"Oh dear, it's not what I meant. It's just I feel like I'm taking you away from something you love. I don't need a lotta help. Josie comes over or calls every day and often fixes a meal."

Taking her mother by the arm, Catharine walked her carefully into the house. Once inside Catharine broke away, entered the kitchen, and opened the door to the refrigerator.

"Just as I thought: it's filled with TV dinners. Does Josie do the shopping as well?"

"If the weather's bad, but I like to go with her if it's not raining or snowing."

"Snowing? You're usually with me in the winter or with Sarah in Florida."

"Yeah, and I'll miss it. But Sarah's only brought me to Florida three times in ten years. I like Washington when it's cold, but I could never live there like you asked me to."

"Is that what's bothering you, Mama? We can take trips together from here."

"I won't be up to trips much longer. I get stiffer and tireder every day. If I took a trip to Washington now, I couldn'a get out of the car!"

"You need someone with you all of the time. We'll talk about it later."

"Oh, come on. It's too expensive—I can take care of myself," she said.

Catharine backed off the subject, not wishing for an argument. They talked about fifteen minutes, and Catharine kissed her mother good-bye.

"I'll call you every other day, and you have my number." Catharine said. "I haven't made a final decision, but I could be here in June after the semester ends." *It's always the same directions,* she thought.

Catharine understood. Her mother's concern stemmed not only from the job sacrifice but also because it meant no more trips to Washington. However, she didn't see Mama being up to long trips at ninety-three.

❦

Catharine wondered whether unloading on a cat might sound crazy to her seminary friends. She "talked" to Chiro a lot since

Kenji died. She adored his beautiful mane and lionlike face. With a smoky coat, long hair, and large paws, he looked as if he weighed more than twenty pounds. Her fingers swiping over his head reminded her of stroking a rich cashmere sweater. She could feel her body relax.

"What will I do, Chiro? Should I teach at Midland Bible College and give up my tenure at the seminary? It's comfortable here. I enjoy my friends and the Washington culture. I love my work. Why give this up for a tiny college in Pennsylvania?"

She answered her own question. "Mama needs me," she said, adding, "even if I don't think I'll like the change." As if sensing her distress, Chiro snuggled close and purred, getting louder with each comment. It would be like starting over in the past.

"If only I could ask Kenji what to do." She tossed a pillow to his side of the bed. She recognized that she'd been too dependent on him during their marriage.

"I miss him so much! Why did he go jogging in twelve-degree weather? Or would he have had the heart attack anyway? He had no signs of illness, and he was thankful for being so 'incredibly healthy.'"

The uncertainties depressed her. Could his death have been prevented? What if he'd had more frequent checkups? Or a better diet? The questions chased each other through her mind. Now they came only when she awoke at night. His foreboding words, "should something happen to me," haunted her. Had he felt threatened by someone? She told herself to search the Internet to find poisons mimicking a heart attack. But by morning light, her fears seemed preposterous.

She cherished his memory: his laughing eyes, unflappable nature, affection, and positive outlook. Gentle yet strict with

Matt, he'd patiently tolerated her mild ADD and encouraged her education and career.

Catharine awoke from her reverie and buried her face in Chiro's fur as tears trickled down and matted his hair. "We were happy and blessed."

His blue eyes stared into hers as if he understood every word.

"This move will be stressful. What a transition! Like the story of the city mouse and the country mouse," she said to Chiro. "But Mama needs us. And sister Sarah claims her husband needs her."

"I'm the only one available to care for her, which is why I must take this job."

She lay awake, praying and meditating on the pros and cons, until she was ready to make her decision. The next day Catharine called President Kenny, her mother, and Sarah. She would move to Pennsylvania.

୬∬ଌ

With classes finished in June, Catharine got busy sorting items into piles representing throw-outs, giveaways, and items to be packed. Kenji's clothing had long ago been donated to a church community center.

She remembered the heartbreaking day.

"These were my husband's clothes," she'd said to the woman at the desk.

The woman responded with feeling. "I understand. We see this a lot, and it's always hard."

Catharine watched his familiar shirts and suits being laid on a table. She walked over and fondled them as tears washed her face. Going out the glass doors, she kept looking back at them. It felt like she was losing him all over again.

Catharine tackled the four gray filing cabinets in Kenji's office. *Thankfully he wasn't a hoarder, or this would be monumental.* It had been two years since Marti Gaston, his assistant, took his scientific papers to the Physics Institute. She wondered why he hadn't contacted her as he said he would. She'd kept Kenji's published papers; maybe they could shed light on his research. A lot of them discussed the physics of space-time.

She didn't feel motivated to plunge into the thick folders in the last of the file cabinets. Its drawers contained souvenirs, pictures, and personal items stored to contemplate in their senior years—*years that won't happen*, she thought.

Toward the end of July, Catharine stood slumped over the fourth filing cabinet, which held their memories, now meaningless to anyone but herself. The first three metal cabinets stood empty like silent, hulking towers over the once-happy landscape of her life.

In the back of one drawer of mementos, she discovered several large manila envelopes, marked "Journal 1, 2, 3." Inside Journal 1 a title page stated "My Memoirs."

Kenji had worked on these periodically. When he died, all memory of them had disappeared in a cloud of grief. He'd once offered to have her read them. The event seemed like years ago, and she'd been too busy. But for several months before he died, he'd returned to the project. *Why now?* She'd wondered. *It should be a retirement task.*

She pulled out Journal 1 and began to read.

1966, Tokyo, Japan

The 1950s were a tumultuous decade in Japan. My father, Yamashiro Isao, never recovered from the days he spent in prison in his homeland. He had the misfortune of attending graduate school in the United States—in Chicago. This made him a traitor in the eyes of the Japanese government during the war. After being liberated from prison, he came home, only to lose his wife five years later with the birth of a son. She never recovered from the starvation and illness the war had caused and was perhaps too frail to survive the extra bodily burden. It seemed all her life forces went into keeping this child in her alive. His specialness was reinforced by the two older sisters who raised him. That son was me.

In early 1966, my father looked older than his sixty years. I remember him lying on a raised bed in a room dimly lit with an oil lamp on a table next to him. Beside the lamp lay a Bible. His white hair hung loosely around his haggard face. Periodically he turned and coughed into a white rag until he hurt. He was isolated from the rest of the world, and his only visitor outside the family was Edmond Brown, an American with whom he had been doing business for two years as a consultant. He struggled to sit up. He asked his daughter, Akiko-chan, to bring me, Kenji-kun, into the room. I followed her into the darkened room through the low doorway. I was sixteen at the time. I bowed and then stood, shoulders back, before my father.

Continuing in Japanese, Isao said, "Kenji-kun, I know I am dying, and I want you to have a better education than you could get here. Brown-san has offered to take one of my children to America for an education like I had. You are young but the only one who can go. Hana-nei-san is married, and Akiko-nei-san is engaged. I will give Brown-san some money, and you can live with him and his wife, and attend an American high school and college. Will you prepare to leave with Brown-san in two weeks?"

"Yes, Father, I will," I said.

❧

A knock at the door distracted Catharine, and she put the paper back in the envelope to read later. Chiro followed her to the entrance.

"It must be Laitha, coming to help us pack."

She opened the paneled walnut door to a slim and attractive Indian woman, dressed in a printed aqua sari. She wore her black hair in a single braid falling to her waist.

"Hello, Catharine. How is it going?"

"Thank you so much for coming. It's going well. I've been through the last filing cabinet, and we need to put the papers from it in boxes."

"Then let's get started," Laitha said.

The two of them put papers into cardboard boxes as they talked. "How did you and Kenji meet? I know you went to college together, but what was the first meeting like?"

"It happened after my father's first heart attack. He had two. The last one killed him twenty years later. He drove a bus in Baltimore and didn't come home one night after his shift ended. Mama tracked him down at St. Joseph's Hospital. He'd had a heart attack while driving the bus. The condition meant a forced retirement.

"I graduated from high school two months later. We had to sell the Maryland home and move back to the family farm. They used the sale money to send me to the nearest college, Midland Bible College.

"I was glad to be back at our family church. I saw Kenji there for the first time. He sat on the front row, reading his Bible, and I thought him exotically good-looking. Then, guess what? On my first day of college, I spied him in freshman English class. Though extremely shy, I wanted to know him so badly. I sat next to him. I still remember the sensation of blushing, but he didn't even look up. It took two weeks for us to speak. I didn't know then that Japanese men found shyness a positive asset in a female."

"What a romantic story."

Catharine didn't notice that Laitha had packed the journal envelopes at the bottom of one of the boxes, closed it, taped it, and went on to another file drawer. With the cabinet emptied, Catharine realized the memoir had been packed, and there'd be no reading for a while. *It probably isn't new material to me anyway.*

She scheduled the movers for August 3. In the days leading up to the move, Catharine enjoyed five separate celebrations and dinners from friends and coworkers, and she gained five pounds. She would miss the condominium and the ornamental garden, with its walking paths in the parterre surrounding the town houses.

She couldn't picture her Japanese-influenced furniture in the family home; the same was true of the bedroom furniture. *No use for a king-size bed in my future.* She toyed with the idea of selling it. *Would it be closure or just another sad parting?* She looked at the bed and cried.

She dispensed with some of her furniture among friends. "The ginger couch won't fit in Mama's house," she said to herself. But she wanted to keep it, so she planned to store it temporarily in a barnlike outbuilding on the farm. The expensive folding screen would go in the farmhouse.

As Catharine contemplated the destiny of each piece of furniture, she felt less melancholy. The bedroom set went to a friend. She stored the things from Matt's room locally, as he had requested.

Later, she'd find a room near the campus for winter during the week and hire a live-in caregiver for her mother. *Surely in the area of kind Mennonite women, there's someone who would like the job.*

The condo sale went quickly in this coveted area of Washington. Some lifetime government employees grabbed it on first sight. They planned to move in on September 1.

On the last day of July, Laitha and Catharine stood in the kitchen, wrapping glasses in newspapers and taking them one at a time from the cherry cabinets. As Laitha carefully wrapped one, Catharine saw a familiar name on the newspaper Laitha held.

"Stop." She jumped toward Laitha and jerked the paper from her hands.

"Is something wrong? What do you see?"

"The headline—a name—it's an obituary."

Spreading out the paper, Catharine read, "Miles Pollack, age fifty-six, well-known Washington attorney, died of a heart attack at his Bethesda home on Monday."

Stunned, Catharine sat down at the kitchen counter. She put her head down and closed her eyes over the newspaper.

"You know him, I presume?" said Laitha.

Catharine shook her head. "Not really. I never met him. He was Kenji's lawyer." She slammed her right fist down on the counter. "What am I going to do with the letter I was supposed to give him?"

"Letter?"

"Yes, Kenji left me a letter to give to him in two years. The two years are up, and Pollack is dead! I've got to find the letter and read it," she said.

Catharine looked around at the packed boxes. Everything from the bedroom was packed. She remembered taking the letter out of the teak box, but what did she do with it? After mentally chastising herself, she said to Laitha, "It's in there somewhere. I'll find it when I unpack."

CHAPTER 4

Catharine could do little to follow up on Miles Pollack, but she did call his former office. The receptionist told her Pollack's associate, Leona James, would be taking his calls and clients.

"Did Mr. Pollack ever work with the Physics Institute here in Washington?"

"I am not aware he did," she said. "But Mrs. James could tell you."

"I'll call back later," Catharine said.

The mystery will have to hang on for a while, Catharine decided. *There's just too much going on in my life.*

❧

In the morning a call came from Aaron Zadlo.

"So, I hear you will be coming to our fair valley soon. Do you have a date set up?"

"I sure do. The move is scheduled for August third."

He offered to meet Catharine at her mother's house, help her get settled, and then take both of them to lunch.

Catharine and Chiro arrived a few days before the moving van to prepare her mother for the invasion of strangers in her home.

Laitha locked up the condo and had her maid clean up debris the movers had left.

A few days before the move, Catharine took her mother to church for her first time in many months. The Mifflintown Church, a squat, square brick building stood on a hill and looked as it had during her youth.

A friendly greeter named Mary handed them a bulletin and hugged her mother.

"Elizabeth, I am so happy to see you. It's been months since I came to your house," she said to her mother in an excited it's-been-so-long voice.

Mary became even more animated when she learned Catharine was Elizabeth's daughter. Eager to enter the chapel, Catharine listened politely and moved on.

Her heart beat excitedly as she stepped through the double doors and looked around. She saw not one person she remembered. She knew Mr. and Mrs. Holtz had died. They'd helped Kenji through college.

She saw a couple of Asian families in the pews. The church had sponsored a group from Cambodia in the 1970s. Apparently their offspring still attended the church, but she didn't know any of them. She spoke to them later and learned they weren't members. Their grandmother, a pillar in the community, had died, and the rest of the family lived in Maryland. Today, they visited Mifflintown because the church had welcomed their family to the United States in August thirty years ago. A church potluck celebrated their return.

Catharine searched for her old friend, Janice. Upon asking, she learned Janice, now a widow, was with her daughter in another state.

After everyone left, she sat with her mother in the empty sanctuary in meditative silence. Staring at the pulpit, she remembered returning from Baltimore to Juniata County and seeing Kenji here for the first time.

Due to a decrease in enrollment, the church school had shut its doors. The community center for distributing clothing and food had also closed. Catharine left saddened. The people were friendly, but they were strangers with no link to her past. She remembered a much larger attendance. She worried that their family church would soon die out.

ᴶᴾ

Juniata County has many overcast days, and August 3 was one of them. The movers arrived at the farmhouse around ten o'clock in the morning, with Aaron not far behind them.

"Good morning, Cat," he said, using her old nickname. "I see things are getting started."

"Well, almost," she said, coming down the steps toward him.

She walked forward but halted when a huge dog burst from Aaron's truck. Panting and jumping like a released racehorse, it danced up to her with its pink tongue hanging out. The gray beast appeared to be a mixed breed—the size and look of a husky with a bit of wolf mixed in.

"Oh!" She stepped back from the oncoming cyclone with the wagging tail. She put her hands up in time to block its advances before it jumped to her level.

"Logan, no!" yelled Aaron. The animal abruptly stopped and sat in front of her, tail and tongue still wagging; the two of them locked in eye contact.

"I'm sorry. I hope he didn't scare you. He's really very gentle and lovable," said Aaron. "He wouldn't hurt a friend, and he obviously views you as a friend. Logan, this is Catharine; Catharine, this is Logan."

Catharine stepped back again, smiled warily, and said, "Pleased to meet you, Logan." Only then did she look away to Aaron and say, "At least he minds you well."

"Yes, I trained him myself. He's my best friend and companion. Now, what can I do? I can carry in some small things." Turning toward the truck, he said with a nod, "They look ready to go, don't they?"

The two men stood around, drinking coffee from McDonald's containers.

"It's been a long day for them already. They need a break, don't you think?" said Catharine.

The two movers seemed to be discussing the best way to get the larger items up the concrete steps. Finally the men opened the doors to the van. One went inside and pulled out small pieces of furniture, and the other set them on the pavement. They carried the large boxes up the steps and put them in an empty room past the parlor. Aaron helped with small boxes and furniture, and he organized the stacks.

Meanwhile Catharine's mother watched from the living room windows. Chiro sat in his cage in back of the house. He wanted to be part of every activity and cried plaintively until Catharine carried him into the kitchen and provided cat treats and fresh water, while her mother's yellow tabby, Barney, eyed him suspiciously and slunk out the back door.

As each piece came off the truck, she directed the workers to other places for storage. The precious Japanese screen went into the house. The ginger couch went into the barn. She told herself this was temporary. She remembered that her father had stored their upright piano in the barn when they returned from Baltimore, leaving it there until it rotted and the keys fell inside.

One of the last pieces to come off the van was a small nightstand belonging to Kenji. It had come from California with them as part of their first bedroom set nearly thirty years ago. It had been in Kenji's study, and Catharine had forgotten to empty it. Just as she feared, the drawer opened while being carried up the steps, and its paper contents spilled over the ground. Aaron rushed to pick them up, with Catharine behind him.

"I'll get a box or bag to put this stuff in," she said.

Aaron gathered them up while Catharine procured a paper bag from the kitchen pantry. While stuffing the papers in the bag, something resembling a ticket folder fell out. Catharine caught it in midair. *What's this?* She recognized it as a Rail Canada train ticket envelope. Inside she found round-trip ticket stubs from Toronto, Ontario, to Edmonton, Alberta. The dates were in November 2004. She remembered that her husband had taken a two-week business trip to Toronto two months before his fatal heart attack. *But why a ticket to Edmonton? He didn't mention such a trip on his return. And why would he take a train?*

She put the ticket folder back in the paper bag and wondered what else she might find in the collection.

CHAPTER 5

The Rail Canada ticket mystified Catharine, but she didn't know how to follow up on it. Calling the institute could be a mistake. *Had he been working on a clandestine project he couldn't tell me about?* The possibilities disturbed her. Right now the move took up her time and energy.

She unpacked what she would need until November, when she might find a room near the campus to stay during the week.

"When I find a place on campus for the winter, I'll hire a lady to be here during the week," Catharine said.

The furrows between Mama's eyes deepened to a frown. "Why would you do that?"

Catharine couldn't tell whether the question was pretend or whether her mother didn't remember their previous arguments.

"Mama, the winters here are severe. You must have someone with you all the time. I know Josie looks out for you. She's close by but getting old herself. You need healthy meals and laundry and cleaning done. And someone available in an emergency."

"I've been doing my own laundry, meals, and cleaning a long time," she said. "And I've had this Life Alert thing for five years and never used in once."

Catharine knew her mother exaggerated her abilities, but she said nothing.

"Mama, when school starts, I won't have time for housework. I have an office at the college, and I'll have a lot of paper work and study to do."

"I won't have a stranger come in here and wait on me." Mama shuffled off.

Catharine calmly went back to her unpacking.

∂♫♪

A week later preparations moved forward for a family dinner at the farmhouse.

Grace, her mother's sister, had lived with her until she died at eighty-seven. Aunt Grace's son had moved to New York for work, and his daughter, Debbie, had stayed in the area and married. Catharine hadn't seen her second cousin since Debbie was a teenager. Now she was a mother with two small children.

Josie and Jake came from down the road; the pastor and his wife and children, and two other distant cousins attended. Catharine kept the food warm as they waited. Debbie and Jerry Martin and their two boys arrived almost an hour late in a whirlwind of activity.

"Hello, hello." Debbie burst in and hugged everyone as the boys ran through the house. "I can't believe it has been so many years," she said, staring at Catharine. "You look so young. I expected an older woman. These are for you." Debbie handed her a package; it contained two large, white crocheted doilies.

"Why, thank you," said Catharine. "Did you make these?"

"I sure did. Crocheting is my hobby. This is like a welcoming gift."

The young woman had light-brown hair raked back into

a ponytail, which fell to her waist. Stunning aqua-blue eyes and long eyelashes accented a pretty face and made up for her slightly protruding ears. In jeans and a yellow T-shirt, she looked "country."

"I'm tired of getting those kids ready," she said and slumped onto the couch with Jerry. She laughed and talked nonstop about the kids, her and Jerry's work, and how she struggled to get things done. Meanwhile she moved frequently from sitting to lying to doing a yoga position. Catharine suspected she, too, had ADD but the pervasive hyper type males more often experienced.

Grandmother Grace Brubaker's family came from strict Mennonites of the old order, dating back to Switzerland with a couple of bishops thrown in. Both Debbie and Jerry had been raised in this "plain" religion. Catharine noticed Debbie's turquoise necklace and small gold earrings and dress. These indicated "backsliding" from the old order.

Jerry wore the ubiquitous jeans and white T-shirt seen all over the county, but his ornate black cowboy boots set him apart. Disheveled straw-blond hair and regular features in a square face gave him a farm boy look.

Their towheaded boys—Jonas and Zach, ages four and five—looked like twins. They galloped through the house, laughing and yelling while the adults tried to converse.

After dinner, the company migrated to the back porch to sit in aging swing gliders. The boys spotted Mama's cat, Barney, and chased him. Diving after the cat and missing him, they rolled around in the grass. "Hey," Jerry yelled, "you'll get deer ticks! Let's take a walk." He invited the pastor's two older children along.

After they left, the adults relaxed and talked about old times.

When the party was over, Catharine felt like doing some deep breathing.

"What a hurricane my cousins are!" she said to Mama. "But I look forward to knowing them better."

"They have been a big help. Jerry mostly. He does all the maintenance around here."

"What does Debbie do?"

"She's a medical receptionist in Lewistown, but I guess you wonder what she does at home. You saw Jerry does the parenting. Debbie manages to sit still long enough to do beautiful crocheting; she gets immersed in it. Their house is full of it, and she sells some. Otherwise she's disorganized and doesn't get much done at home outside of meals. She's a decent cook. The place is a mess every time I've seen it. But she plays with the kids, and they love it. She's like a kid herself."

✥

Mexico, Pennsylvania, sounded familiar; it was her Aunt Ella's birthplace. The farm in Mexico was one of several her grandfather had leased and worked before he settled at the family farm near Richfield. In those days he'd traveled to Florida to pick oranges during winters.

The local radio station, located near Mexico, sat in the middle of a large field under its towering antenna The manager called her for an interview in mid-August.

A pleasant older man with a "radio" voice did the interview in his small, compact studio.

"Today on WMBC radio we will be talking to Dr. Catharine Weaver Yamashiro, who has returned to Juniata County after being gone for thirty-five years. Dr. Yamashiro will be the new professor of biblical languages and theology at our own Midland Bible College.

"Thank you for being with us, Dr. Yamashiro."

"Thank you for inviting me."

"So you're a native of our area; Yamashiro is not a Juniata County name," he said, laughing.

"No, my husband was a student from Japan at Midland Bible College when I met him. My Weaver family goes back seven generations in Pennsylvania, most of them in this county. But I was born in Baltimore, where my father drove a bus for twenty-years before we moved back to the farm where he grew up. He inherited the farm after his parents died. I was a baby, so I grew up here until age thirteen, when we returned to Baltimore. The farm wasn't generating enough for me and my sister to go to college. Daddy got his old job back, but unfortunately he had a heart attack five years later while I was in my senior year of high school. He had to retire, because the Baltimore transit system didn't allow drivers to continue after a heart attack."

"And you came back to Pennsylvania?"

"We came back, and I attended Midland Bible College, where I met my husband, Kenji. My father lived seventeen more stress-free years in this beautiful county and rented out the farmland. After graduation Kenji and I married and finished most of our graduate work in California."

"I understand you taught biblical languages and got your PhD at the prestigious Methodist Seminary in Washington, DC, where you lived for years. Isn't this a difficult transition from the city to Juniata County?"

"Yes, my husband died two years ago. He was a physicist working in DC. As a widow with my mother here in Richfield, it was time to come home. I appreciate the quietness of the country and the joy of walking in nature. It brings back many memories, like hiking up on Black Log Mountain."

Catharine sat up straight and reached her arms out in a stretch.

Her tension disappeared. The announcer relaxed in his office chair. They continued the interview by discussing the courses she would be teaching and her approach to them.

"What are your plans for living in the country again? Are you with your mother?"

"Oh, yes. It's so wonderful to live with her again. I did bring her to Washington most winters, but she never got used to the city. Being home is heaven this time of year. The fields and forests are so green. I'm motivated to plant a garden every year. I guess it's too late for this year."

The announcer laughed. "You may change your mind about a garden when you see what happens to it."

"What?"

"The deer population has grown since you lived here. We need six-foot-high fences to protect gardens. Plus other wildlife have multiplied like raccoons, ground hogs, and rabbits. And bears have moved down from the mountains. They have been known to invade homes."

"Oh, it's something I'll have to deal with, I guess. But I love animals more than gardens."

They both laughed as Catharine threw up her hands in a gesture of surrender.

CHAPTER 6

In August the TV news reminded them of the third anniversary of the Hurricane Katrina disaster, and Catharine wondered what the rest of the hurricane season through November might mean for her sister in Florida.

August ended with hot, humid air still hanging over Juniata County. Summer didn't want to leave, but cooler air convinced it to loosen its sweaty hands and slip away as September moved in. Aaron introduced her to two of his friends, Kris and Erika, two married teachers, and they went hiking together in the mountains one Sunday.

The campus awakened from its summer silence two weeks before college opening day. Catharine attended meetings with her department, met her colleagues, and set up her office. Her office was located across the hall from the classroom where she would teach. It contained a computer and all the accessories needed for her specialized teaching. Her predecessor, Dr. Costello, had left them when he moved to Seattle.

Dr. Costello had taken a more lucrative position there, since he had a young, growing family. She contacted him for more insight on teaching at Midland's Religion Department, and he graciously answered her questions.

Catharine wanted to avoid interjecting her personal theology into the history curriculum yet introduce young minds to fresh ideas. She learned Dr. Costello hadn't been a cookie-cutter theology teacher. He believed the school allowed room for adapting ancient Scripture to new scholarship without taking textual criticism beyond evangelical boundaries. Most important, she wanted the students to think for themselves and not just reflect someone else's ideas. The students came from evangelical churches, mostly Baptist and Mennonite.

During an intensive summer at a Michigan seminary a year ago, Catharine had enjoyed taking classes from a highly respected Hebrew scholar and felt his knowledge could be integrated into the nondenominational history course. He had studied the subject both as a Jew and a Christian convert. His insights came from inside the Hebrew mind. She hadn't realized at the time how important the course would be in her future.

The first day of school was scheduled for mid-September, with thirty students in each Hebrew Bible history class and twenty in the Hebrew language class. It would be a time of getting acquainted with students and other teachers. Everything was new, and Catharine felt like an outsider. She was sure most of this was in her mind and not reality. Aaron made up for this by inviting her out to lunch or dinner on Sundays. When Mama was up to it, she came along. Mama frequently complained of being tired. For the last several years, she often fell asleep when she sat still for more than fifteen minutes.

Catharine wanted to keep her relationship with Aaron on a friend basis, so she insisted they each pay for their own meals. She explained to him, "After all, we both make similar salaries, and it wouldn't seem fair if you played the outdated role of the man paying for every occasion." He agreed.

Catharine became nervous while anticipating opening day. The butterflies in her stomach increased as the first day of class drew nearer. She arrived at her office before seven o'clock in the morning, and the first class was at eight. She piled everything she needed on the desk. Her familiar briefcase sat in front of her like a security blanket. She turned in the swivel chair to stare out the window while praying to connect with her students. She wouldn't have difficulty with the subject material. But she had always taught it to serious theology students with definite goals.

A knock at the door caused her to turn around. Aaron entered and said, "I just wanted to give you some support. I figured you would be nervous before your first class. I know I am. The first day of school from first grade forward has always made me nervous."

"You are so perceptive," she said, smiling.

"I thought you might want me to pray with you."

"Oh, thank you, Aaron."

After a comforting and brief prayer, he took her hand and squeezed it. "Go get 'em, girl!" And he left.

Catharine felt calmer, but the rapid heartbeat continued.

After several minutes, she heard a jangling bell blasting down the hall and the sound of footsteps and talking as students entered the classroom across the hall.

This would be the Hebrew language class. The history class would begin at nine, followed by the daily chapel period at ten and the second history class at eleven. She crossed the hard vinyl floor covering as it reflected the sound of her high heels. The classroom seemed large for the twenty registered students. She saw only one female in the group.

Standing before them, Catharine relaxed, feeling at home behind the familiar pulpit. She introduced herself and learned many had heard the radio interview the college PR Department announced in advance by e-mail to the students. Then she invited the students to introduce themselves and say why they were taking the class.

Most of the Hebrew class included theology majors who hoped to become pastors or teachers. Some were recent converts to evangelical Christianity, still in their first love for God. They would be like infants in the faith, with only a year or two of Bible college experience. Two of them introduced themselves as veterans of the Iraq war, returning to college for training to serve their Lord.

The Old Testament history students streamed in as soon as the first class vacated the room. This larger class represented a broader selection of students who had chosen it as an elective. Some said they had chosen the class as a result of the radio interview.

CHAPTER 7

In early October, Catharine wrote in her journal,

It's rained off and on for days and been cloudy for a month. But today I woke up to blue skies, and the rain-washed colors outside sparkled. A light frost on October first invited in masses of yellow, orange, and golden colors on the lower mountains. "I'm beginning to like this place," I said to Chiro. "It's a day to spend in God's sanctuary."

I put Chiro in his carrier, and we rode around the countryside, stopping here and there. The drive down Route 35 cut through blocks of brilliantly colored trees, harvested wheat fields, drying cornfields, and green meadows spreading across the countryside and reaching up over the mountains with deep-green pine and spruce forests, all coming together like one of those colorful Mennonite quilts the women make when they get together for their weekly quilting parties.

In the evening Catharine made a list of people to contact from the past. She didn't realize what a Pandora's box some of them would open up. Nevertheless, her active mind spun out of control as she conjured up numerous activities and interests to follow up on without considering the time involved.

Finding the family who had taken Kenji in after he left the Browns was at the top of her list. She knew Edmond Brown had kept the money Kenji's father gave him for the trip. Instead of flying him to America, Brown had put him on a cargo ship to Los Angeles and paid for a bus ticket to Lewistown, Pennsylvania. The Browns had made Kenji work long hours on their estate. Their son, Joe, about Kenji's age, had been a caustic bully. After Edmond Brown became violent, Kenji escaped and contacted a Seventh-day Adventist pastor in the next town. This was the Christian religion his father had studied before he died, and his children had chosen to be baptized into the faith.

The pastor found Kenji a home with a Mennonite farm family named Yoder, and he attended public high school and Midland Bible College. Members of his church had assisted with tuition and expenses to supplement work on the Yoder farm.

Catharine considered contacting the Browns to see whether there were any family members left but changed her mind.

Other plans included visits to the Mennonite church her father had attended as a child. Because of the shunning, her father hadn't been allowed to eat with the family during his visits home, but his children and spouse could join them since they had never been Mennonite.

She hoped to spend time with her cousins, Debbie and Jerry, and invite them and the children for family meals; she wanted to teach a Bible study class at her church and visit the county Mennonite Historical Center close to the farm on Route 35. Plans needed to be made for a class tour of the Mennonite Visitor's Center in Lancaster, where they exhibited a replica of the Old Testament wilderness tabernacle.

Catharine listed personal errands, such as shopping for heavy winter clothing and snow boots, and doing genealogical research. She couldn't wait to visit the scenic parks to the north and State College, its shops, and Penn State activities. Maybe she'd even take classes there.

On the margins of her thoughts she hoped Aaron might accompany her on some of these trips. *Don't make such plans,* she told herself. *You could be disappointed.* Nevertheless, she couldn't help remembering him with a smile.

ꝯꝯ

On Sunday morning Aaron called to invite her for a ride to the parks north of the county. The trip included Logan, the first time she'd seen him since the move.

When she opened the door, Logan jumped to her eye level with a furiously wagging tail; then he placed large, wet, leaf-covered paws on her shoulders. Catharine stepped back into the room. "Get him off me!" she said.

"No, stop," Aaron yelled to the dog. Logan sat down immediately.

Catharine tried to follow her initial shocked response with pretend calmness as if this were an ordinary welcome experience.

"I'm sorry," he said. "Here I am, apologizing for Logan again."

"That—that's all right," she said, wiping the leaves from her jacket while keeping eye contact with those large brown eyes, which she admitted did look friendly.

Suddenly from behind her came an ear-piercing scream ending in a growl—then an unearthly guttural sound. Chiro stood in the middle of the hallway with hair sticking out all over him. Catharine had never seen him this way. Then they heard hisses and more screaming growls.

It was as if Logan couldn't believe his eyes as his head jerked forward. Before Aaron could grab him, the dog bounded down the hall after the large, fluffed ball.

"No. Stop." Aaron leaped after him, and Catharine followed.

Chiro stood his ground for a split second, then ran for the kitchen with the parade behind him. They ran past the parlor and turned right at the kitchen. By the time Aaron and Catharine got there, Chiro had jumped on the kitchen counter and slid into a box of cereal, exploding it all over the floor. Chiro dashed down the counter, shot up on the refrigerator, and stood growling and spitting.

Logan stood at the bottom, barking in a deep voice.

"Stop," Aaron yelled again. Logan sat instantly, shut up, and stared wide eyed at the performance above him. "Out, Logan," his master said sternly, pointing to the door; the beast twisted his body around and took leave of his audience.

Chiro calmed down and immediately vaulted to the counter and on the linoleum floor as if he'd never been afraid. But now he stalked Aaron and Logan to the door like prey. Logan didn't look back, his head down in shame.

Man and dog stayed on the porch, while Catharine cleaned up. Chiro didn't hide but sat and stared at the closed door, as if challenging the duo to come back.

After petting Chiro, Catharine reassured him, "I will never let the monster in here again to frighten you." She got her bag and went out the door to join Aaron in the car.

They drove south into the country and west through Lewistown, taking Route 22 up into the mountains toward State

College. "You remember Alan Seeger National Park in the Seven Mountains area?" he asked.

"Daddy took us to the hemlock forests many times. After he retired, he liked to ride around the area. In college we went for rides in groups. Don't you remember? You often went along."

The mountains got higher, and Aaron turned left into the park. The truck bumped over an unpaved road deep into the woods past roaring streams and thick, green clumps of rhododendron bushes. After about forty minutes, they entered the hemlock forest, and Aaron parked in an empty lot under the giant hemlocks.

"What a scene!" Catharine said.

Sunlight filtered through lacy branches. A waterfall on one side spilled clear water down multicolored rocks. The two took a path through a tunnel of rhododendron bushes, then followed a trail through dense hemlock groves and over narrow bridges. The forest was silent, except for cawing crows high in the trees. They circled back to the entrance after an hour's walk.

Aaron retrieved a red lunch cooler from the truck and spread out a checkered green oil cloth over a picnic table. He took out sandwiches, fruit, and water. He looked up suddenly and caught her watching him. She looked away, then glanced back. "Did anyone ever tell you that you look like Adrien Brody, the actor?" she said.

"You mean, the guy in *The Pianist*? Actually, yes. After it came out, I had several people mention it. I guess because of the nose." He laughed.

"Yes, but his nose is larger, and you have curly hair. But more around the eyes." She noticed his brown eyes with speckles of green and blue. Most people would call them hazel.

"I take it as a compliment," he said.

"It was meant to be."

"Enjoy your chicken sandwiches," he said. "I made them myself."

"Chicken?" she said. "I'm so sorry. I thought you knew I'm a vegetarian."

"Uh-oh. I should have remembered you don't order meat at restaurants."

Catharine was sorry she had mentioned it and tried to backtrack.

"I eat chicken occasionally," she said, taking a bite. "Did you know chickens think?"

"Think?" he said.

"Yes, I read online that researchers have discovered that chickens have a language among themselves, with different clucks meaning different things. Researchers said they seem to use their brains to make decisions and communicate."

"And that bothers you about eating them?"

"Somewhat."

"You're funny, Cat. But I like your sensitivity," he said. "I'll remember next time, but enjoy your lunch for now. Pretend it's tofu."

She was already looking forward to a next time.

The three of them had walked miles that day, and they finished their lunch in the hemlock forest with no more than a tail wag from Logan. They returned along the same scenic route, while Logan rode with his head out the back window.

"That could be dangerous for him," said Catharine.

"Isn't everything in life that's fun a bit dangerous?" Aaron replied.

Catharine didn't answer but wondered why such an innocent remark caused her heart to skip a beat.

CHAPTER 8

Unsettling things happened in the fall. By November the trees were mostly bare, with a few dried brown leaves clinging to their skeletons. Feathery gray hills crept up to dark-green spruce, hemlock, and pine on the mountains. Winter cold would soon climb over the mountains and into their valley, accompanied by shorter sunlit days. To Catharine, winter's only redeeming features were Thanksgiving and Christmas. She looked forward to the pre-Christmas concerts at the college, with its many talented musicians.

On an overcast day in mid-November, Catharine returned to her office after the third class. An envelope lay in the middle of her desk with "Mrs. Yamashiro" handwritten on it. *What's this?* she thought.

Opening the envelope, she saw the message scrawled on a lined yellow sheet.

Why did you come back here? Your Jap husband
killed my grandfather. You are going to pay.

Catharine dropped the letter, horrified. She read it again and again. *Who had done this? Why would they do this? Some sort of prank? No, grandfather intimated something of long ago.* There was no doubt it talked about Kenji.

Should she call the police? Tell Aaron? She sat down, not so much scared as puzzled. Had something happened here years ago she didn't know about? No, Kenji wouldn't have killed anyone, but why did this kid—she was sure it was a kid based on the language and handwriting—think so? If he's delusional, she wouldn't want him arrested. He needed help. She put the letter in her briefcase and went home early to think about what to do.

Driving to the farmhouse, Catharine barely noticed the orange and pink clouds reflecting the setting sun and the ribbons of azure-blue sky around them.

In the rearview mirror she saw a dull, red pickup. Was it following her? She went right on a side road at McAlisterville. It didn't turn. After a short distance, she turned around in the driveway of a duplex and drove back to Route 35, then home.

At least once a week, Catharine dreamed of Kenji. She saw him alive, well, and young. In her dream they lived in a house in California she didn't recognize; Matt was a toddler in a room filled with toys. In other dreams they were driving across the country to California through flat deserts, forests, and snow-covered, rocky mountains. The dream was in living, beautiful color, and she was happy. Catharine analyzed the dreams as a desire to return to their youthful days on the West Coast.

But this night her dreaming took a dark turn. Driving her car, she saw an old red truck beside her. She couldn't see the driver, but Kenji sat in the passenger seat. She crossed a bridge over water, more like the ocean than a river. Her car veered off the bridge and dropped below; the red truck followed her into the water. Next she was swimming. She looked for the truck, but it disappeared below the waves. She awakened, frightened. It was six o'clock in the morning.

Catharine lay abed, thinking about the dream. She got up slowly for morning devotions—a Bible promise from the porcelain box Laitha had given her years ago, a Bible reading, and a meditation based on the Lord's Prayer. Then she showered and dressed.

Chiro vocalized his demand as soon as she stepped from the room. After he ate, they walked. Chiro trotted beside her on the asphalt. "It's a chilly morning, so we won't stay out long," she told him.

For years Catharine had followed a strict health routine as part of her ADD therapy. She blended a smoothie: a mixture of greens, blueberries, banana, protein powder, and almond milk. Then she prepared her mother's breakfast.

"Good morning, Mama." Catharine entered her mother's room with a bowl of oatmeal, fruit, and a warm drink.

"Good morning, my dear," Mama said. "I'm really loving this attention."

"I'm leaving now. I want you to have a beautiful day," Catharine said, kissing her mother on the forehead.

Outside, Catharine looked around; there was no red truck on the highway this morning.

All during the drive, she focused on the letter while going past the fields, past Richfield, past McAlisterville, and through Mifflintown. She climbed the mountain road leading to the campus, still thinking about it. The road wound between strips of green and brown fields; the rolling, undulating hills made her lean to the left. The road reminded her to find a rental before winter snows made the trip dangerous.

As soon as classes ended, she notified the department secretary and left for Lewistown, a small city to the northwest. She parked near the offices of the *Lewistown Sentinel*, and inside, a young, dark-haired woman named Lilly showed her to the archives. For an hour Catharine perused papers from 1966 to 1967; then she found it: FOREIGN STUDENT WITNESSES FATAL FALL.

> Kenji Yamashiro, a visiting student from Japan who had lived at the house, had come back to pick up some items he had left. As he approached the house, he saw the owner, Edmond Brown, and his son, Joe, doing repair work on the third-floor balcony, when the elder Brown apparently slipped and reached out to his son but slid into the balcony railing. The damaged railing broke through, and he fell to the ground. Yamashiro said Brown was unconscious, and he immediately called an ambulance from a phone inside the house. Brown's wife wasn't home at the time. Brown died of a brain hemorrhage later that day at the Lewistown Hospital.

Catharine copied the report. The letter writer, she decided, must be Edmond Brown's grandson, and for some unknown reason he held Kenji responsible for Edmond's death. *He needs to see the newspaper account*, she thought.

She showed the article to Lilly on the way out and asked whether she had heard of the Brown family.

"I heard about the accident years later. I was told Mrs. Brown, Joe's wife, lives with her son, Ralph, in the old house, and it's a bit run down. It's on the other side of town, but I don't know where," Lilly said.

There was one other place to look. *Kenji's viewpoint of the accident must be in his memoir.*

CHAPTER 9

As Catharine parked her Camry, her mother called from the porch. "You're home early. Is anything wrong?"

"No, Mama. I left early to do some research in Lewistown," she said, running up the steps two at a time.

Her mother rose from her rocking chair; using her cane, she hobbled into the house with her daughter.

"Josie came over and shared a lunch she made, and I'm not ready for supper."

"Good. I have to get into some of my boxes. I didn't want to disturb them before I moved near the campus next month."

Her mother turned away, muttering. Again Catharine explained to her, "I know this is our home, but you can't be alone here at your age, and I have to get to work every day. It's only for about four months. I'll come home on weekends when the roads are safe."

She continued, "I heard from a woman yesterday who has a cottage to rent on the campus, and it has an extra bedroom. I'd like you to stay with me there during the winter. What would you think of that?"

"I've been here for many winters, and I don't need to move," she said, striking the floor with her cane as she headed for her rocker in the kitchen.

Catharine frowned.

Chiru followed Catharine to the storage room. "You're always where the action is," she said. She felt overwhelmed as she eyed the stacks of boxes. Chiro jumped to the lowest one, then worked his way up to the highest.

"How will I find the box with those numbered brown envelopes?" she said to herself and Chiru.

She had neglected to write the contents on the boxes Laitha packed. She began opening one box after another.

"I can't lift those book boxes. I hope the journal box isn't under one of them."

She opened six accessible boxes and rummaged through them. The seventh one was topped off with recognizable souvenirs. She dug down to the bottom till her hand touched a large envelope, and she pulled it out. "Journal 1" was printed on the front.

"I found them!"

On the last page, Kenji said he still worked at Brown's. She laid the journal aside and dove for the next envelope, "Journal 2." It began with Kenji's escape from the Brown mansion the day after both father and son beat him.

> That night I was too sore to sleep with bruises evident all over my body. I had been kicked numerous times and hit in the face. One side of my face was lacerated and an eye blackened. I didn't go out the next morning to feed the animals. At about 7:00 a.m., banging at my door woke me; I heard curses accompanied by demands that I go to work.

"I cannot come out," I said. "I think some of my bones are broken." To my observation this wasn't true.

The reply was a round of more cursing, footsteps stomping down the hall, then silence. No one came back the rest of the day. By dark I was hungry with only a few crackers in my room. I wondered what they might do to me next. It was time to leave.

I had practiced climbing out the bedroom window if I should ever need to. There was a tree limb close to the window. I learned to grab the limb with my hands and throw my legs over it. Then hand over hand, I could get to the trunk and shimmy down. I had done it enough times at night to make it easy when I was in good health. But what about now? I packed one small suitcase, tied it with rope I had taken from the shop, and carefully lowered it from the window. It was about midnight, and the house was quiet.

I crawled out the window and grabbed the branch, but when I swung my body up, the pain seemed unbearable. I couldn't help myself; I made a low cry. I waited for the dogs to bark. They hadn't done so on previous climbs, because they knew me as a friend who fed and petted them. I clenched my jaw and slowly crawled to the tree. Once there I stopped to listen. Nothing stirred. I went down the tree, but close to the bottom, I fell with a thud. Still nothing. I grabbed the suitcase and ran for the woods. I looked back from the woods in time to see a light go on somewhere in the house. Frightened, I ran and walked what seemed like miles into the woods before coming out the other side where a bridge crossed a small river. I hid under the bridge until daylight. I began the day by bathing in the cold creek, but at least I had soap and a washcloth.

Fortunately, I had hidden a moderate amount of money my father gave me in Japan. The bus trip to Lewistown had given me opportunity to exchange it for American money. I'd hid it well in a space under the bathtub in my room along with my visa and other identity papers. I saw evidence my room had been searched, but they didn't find the money. I took out three dollars and decided to eat in town. It was a two-mile walk, and I was sore and weak. But I was free, and I went to breakfast. I must have looked like a wounded soldier as I entered the café.

The waitress looked sympathetic and asked what happened to me. I told her a drunk friend had accidentally hit me last night. She said no more but served me my first satisfying meal in America.

The Browns never allowed me to attend church, but on a trip for supplies once, I'd noticed a Seventh-day Adventist church in the next town. I had memorized how to get there and determined to find it. I discovered from the waitress that a bus from Lewistown went through Mifflintown every morning to take workers into Harrisburg. I walked as fast as my sore legs could take me to the bus stop down the street. It seemed as if God was directing me because I got there in time to board the bus, and the driver was willing to stop at the church.

It was another small but important miracle to find the pastor at the church on his day off. He knelt in prayer at the front of the sanctuary. He later told me he'd pastored three churches and was preparing to visit shut-ins who lived in Mifflintown.

I referred to my well-used Japanese-English dictionary many times during our conversation. I explained who I was and how I'd gotten to Pennsylvania. To allay my fears of the Browns finding me, he told me they could be arrested for abusing me.

I stayed with the pastor, his wife, and their four children for a week in their small house. I shall always be thankful for their care and hospitality. The pastor found a Christian family with a large house on a farm outside Mifflintown. The Yoders offered me room and board in exchange for some farm work, and I could attend the local public high school.

All wasn't over with the Browns. In November, after school had started, Mr. Yoder offered to take me to Lewistown to retrieve the rest of my clothes. We parked a ways from the house to avoid having Pa Yoder involved should an argument break out. As I walked to the house, I could see Edmond and his son, Joe, on the third-story balcony. Since they were dressed in work clothes, I assumed they were doing repairs. As I came closer, I could see they were arguing. I saw Edmond hit his son in the face. At the same time, he slipped and started to slide toward the railing and reached out to his son. Joe didn't take his hand. The elder Brown continued his slide, hitting the railing and cracking the ancient wood. He went through it and fell with a thud on the cement below.

I ran up to the house where he lay. He was unconscious. I ran through the open door to the wall phone and called the emergency number for an ambulance. Mrs. Brown had placed the emergency list next to the phone only recently. I was thankful.

"Well," said Catharine, then gave an audible gasp. She lay down the sheet of paper. Kenji had told her about the Browns. "But this is much worse than I thought," she said. Her eyes watered. She placed the papers back in the brown envelope but not before noticing the next page; instead of being page twenty, it jumped to page thirty-four. She thought the number jump was curious, but other things on her mind kept her from looking for the missing pages.

CHAPTER 10

The days grew shorter as a gloomy mid-November approached. Catharine and Aaron often accompanied their hiking buddies, Kris and Erika, to new trails in neighboring counties. She met Aaron for lunch in the cafeteria most days and looked forward to their conversations. She reminded herself not to let them get too personal. He was her intellectual equal, and they shared broad interests about everything from astronomy to zoology.

Very often their conversation turned toward the earth's origins. As a scientist, Aaron appeared to believe in Darwinian evolution though he'd never stated this. "The literal biblical concept," he said, "is based on a world view nothing like ours. It's out of sync with everything we know about geological layers and dating methods. The biblical writers believed in a flat earth with a dome covering it. How could that fit in our cosmos?"

"I know that, but there are better ways to interpret the creation story besides macro-evolution. How can you claim any theory true or false if science is based on observation?" Catharine said. "Truth is not always available in measurable facts. Some stop believing, claiming honesty led them away. Can we be honest about our knowledge in this vast cosmos? God is a mystery, but

He couldn't create with violence and death over long eons and call it good. It would be against His character. God doesn't exist in human time, and we don't know the mysteries of time or space. I learned that from my husband. That's why we shouldn't claim days were the same length then as now. It would be saying something that isn't in the Bible. We know they are different on other planets. That could explain the long lifetimes noted before the deluge that destroyed life as it was then."

"Perhaps," said Aaron, "the creation story is what God revealed to humans in their unscientific world view. Why did they need scientific facts? His objective was to give them spiritual knowledge. The story meant God created."

"A good point," Catharine said. "Well, enough for now. But I need to talk to you about something else."

She decided to tell him about Ralph Brown.

"What do you think of this?" she said, pulling the note from her purse. "It was left on my desk nearly two weeks ago."

Aaron read it and looked alarmed. "This should be reported to the police."

"But it's no doubt a kid who's gotten wrong information. In fact, I am rather sure I know who it is and what's behind it."

She explained Kenji's arrival in Pennsylvania in 1966 and his mistreatment at the hand of the Browns, his escape, and his witnessing the accident from the street when Edmond Brown fell and died. She told him about the newspaper report.

Aaron frowned. "It sounds like Ralph Brown's father must have told him Kenji caused the accident when it was actually him. There is either a lot of denial or guilt. Is the father still living?"

"I don't think so. The receptionist said she lived alone with her son in the old house."

"I'll go with you to the sheriff," Aaron said. "I know him

personally, and he should be aware of this. Maybe you should have someone keep a close check on your house."

"Except for the first day, when I was on edge anyway and thought I was being followed by a red truck, nothing unusual has happened. I went down another road and wasn't followed, so it was just my nerves. How would he even know where I live?

"But Aaron, I have some other news for you. Mrs. Koster, who has the large estate near the campus on Blueberry Lane, came to see me at my office. She heard I needed a winter place. Old Mrs. Miller, who rented her cottage, moved to the Lutheran Home. She offered the cottage to me, and I said yes."

"Great! Is your mom going to move with you?"

"She won't leave her house, so I've got to find a full-time caregiver for the winter. I would prefer someone to move in if I could find her. I'm going to check at my church, but I don't think there's anyone who does caregiving. Oh, there might be some older women, but I want someone younger and stronger."

"Are you going to put an ad in the local papers? I'd put an ad in Lewistown too."

"Yes, I'll do it. If I don't find someone soon, I won't be able to leave my mother alone at the house, especially with this boy threatening me."

Catharine continued, "Anyway, *cottage* conjures up pictures of a tiny, cozy house from a fairy tale. I can picture an old-fashioned setting of lampstands with doilies, a lace tablecloth, a fireplace, and a mahogany armoire—maybe kind of Victorian."

"I'm going to see the cottage now. You can come with me if you like," she added.

They walked through the campus to Blueberry Lane, followed the circular driveway, and turned down a gravel road. About half a mile down on the left, they saw an iron-gate entrance to the Koster estate and a three-story, massive stone-and-brick house, probably from the late 1800s. Its decorative half-timbering categorized it as a Tudor-inspired structure with chimneys and leaded-glass casement windows. Vines crawled up the sides, and a couple of turrets gave it an ancient feel. This time of year the house looked sad and dark.

When they knocked at the door, Mrs. Koster answered and invited them in. Catharine noticed her questioning look at Aaron.

"This is Aaron Zadlo who teaches at the school. He was kind enough to walk me over and give me his opinion," said Catharine.

"Oh," she said, "I didn't think the place was for a couple." And she laughed while Catharine turned bright red.

Miriam Koster proved to be a pleasant person, who frequently smiled and laughed. Gray-haired with hazel eyes in a narrow face, she was thin and tall, and wore a navy pantsuit. Catharine pictured the woman wearing an elegant dress, drinking tea, and entertaining guests in this glorious house. She lived on the estate with her husband, a retired math professor. A wealthy ancestor, who helped found the college in the mid-1800s, had built the house.

After discussing rent and related topics, Miriam led them through a long hallway, out a back door, and down a brick walkway to a small, gray stone cottage sitting among spruce and pine trees. Expecting a contemporary wooden structure, Catharine was surprised because the cottage looked like it predated the estate house. A narrow gravel road, branching off the main driveway, ended under a metal-roofed carport. They entered through a heavy wooden door opening directly into a small parlor. A modern oak counter divided the living space from the kitchen and eating area. From the kitchen, a hall led to a second entrance and the carport. Shelves on either side of the hall served as a pantry.

Large, updated windows had been added at the back, where a writing desk faced the woods. Left of the parlor was a small room with a twin bed across from a bathroom. Behind it was the main bedroom, which contained a full-sized bed, a nightstand, two dressers, and a closet. The rooms felt cozy but in need of decorating. Beautiful but bare antique pieces furnished the cottage. Even the bed displayed a high wooden headboard of carved flowers.

The windows had old-fashioned pulldown blinds.

"Well, look at that," Catharine said. The blinds in the bedroom had painted scenery on them, and she thought of the screens her sister had painted years ago.

"The furniture came from the main house and has been in the family for generations," Miriam said. "With only the two of us, we closed most of the rooms and moved some of the furniture here. When we were younger, we rented rooms to married students. I'm getting a new mattress for the bed, but I think everything else is supplied. You'll want curtains and a few things to make it homey. We plan to paint the walls. Do you have a favorite color, Catharine?"

"Actually, yes. I'd like a pale yellow or ivory," Catharine said.

She was surprised when Aaron suggested ivory would fit better with other colors. *Why should the color matter to him? He isn't going to live here!* she thought.

Catharine felt a mixture of resentment that he should make her decision, yet there was a kind of excitement that he might want to visit her. Later in the day, she twirled the conversation around in her head and wondered whether it was a red flag that he might be bossy in a relationship.

The next day Aaron called Sheriff Zephaniah Talkin and made an appointment with him in Mifflintown. His office sat across from the county's domed administration building.

"Zeph, this is Catharine Yamashiro, who teaches at MBC. She has an incident to tell you about," said Aaron when they entered the sheriff's office.

"Hello, Sheriff Talkin," said Catharine.

"Come in," the sheriff said. "Please call me Zeph." Zeph looked shorter than one would expect for a man of the law. He was also wide with a double chin and a rosy, round face. Catharine showed him the note and told the story about her husband's experience. She asked him to read the newspaper article from 1966.

"Lewistown isn't my district, so I don't know the Browns," Zeph said. "But I'll do some checking. For now, if you notice anything suspicious, call right away. Call 9-1-1 if it looks like an emergency. But there isn't much we can do unless he makes a move to harm or stalk you. We really don't have evidence he wrote the letter at this point. I'll have my boys drive up to Richfield and look around your house as part of their night patrol."

They drove back to the college parking lot, and Catharine picked up her car and went home, aware of every vehicle on the road.

The search for a suitable caregiver wasn't easy. Debbie and Jerry were no help, but Jerry promised to use her father's old tractor to keep the snow plowed, and he would continue to do necessary maintenance. Debbie did have names to suggest, but each proved to be either uninterested or unsuitable. A newspaper ad brought in several inquiries, resulting in five interviews. None of them fit Catharine's high standards.

Catharine prayed for the right person. Right before Thanksgiving, she got an answer to her ad in the Lewistown paper. A woman with experience and references called. Her name was Rose Lauver, and she was willing to stay overnight during the week. The price was higher than Catharine had anticipated, but after the interview, she hired Rose on the spot.

When Catharine's mother met Rose a day later, the expected argument didn't materialize. "Mama responded to Rose's affirmations and attentiveness positively," she told Aaron. "Rose is so amicable and friendly. I think I made the right choice."

"Well, if she is all of those things, she will be great," said Aaron.

December 1 was set for her move.

CHAPTER 11

Thanksgiving came with a nostalgic dinner planned at Jacob's Farm. Catharine and Debbie put together the traditional turkey dinner—at least Catharine did, while Debbie chattered.

"I can't wait to meet your boyfriend," she said with a teenage giggle.

"Please call him a friend," Catharine said. "Boyfriend is not where we are at."

"Well, I hope you get there soon." She giggled again. "There's nothing like being in love." She pretended a swoon.

"Now, Debbie, don't embarrass me by making our friendship anything more than it is when you meet him, okay?"

"I promise," she said.

Debbie had made two pumpkin pies and one apple pie, and their aroma flooded the house, reminding them of Thanksgivings past.

"I have to hand it to you, Debbie. You can make pies. The apple one has so many apples packed in it, and the crust is so high—it's huge! I'm not much of a cook these days. But I'll make Mama's cottage cheese loaf and walnuts for the vegetarians. I've got it down pat."

Mama shuffled into the kitchen. The joy on her face gave both of them a rest from the harried rush. "Mama, you look so happy," said Catharine.

"I am," she said and laughed. She petted Barney, who had jumped up on a stool to get attention.

The loaf and vegetables were barely finished when the first guests arrived. Mildred and Sally, two eighty-five-year-olds from the Mifflintown church, had come in Mildred's old Dodge. An older couple from Richfield, Mr. and Mrs. Soren, were next. Jerry moved in from the porch, bringing Aaron with him. "This young man just showed up on our doorstep, asking for something to eat," said Jerry. "Does anybody know him?"

Everyone laughed, and Catharine introduced her "friend and work colleague" to the group. Jonas and Zach came tromping in, already acquainted with Aaron, having run to his truck when he drove in.

"These little guys are a great welcoming party," said Aaron.

These new relationships showed another dimension of Aaron as being more playful than Catharine had seen. He joked easily with Debbie and Jerry, and played with the boys throughout the evening.

The only awkward moment happened when everyone quieted down at the table while eating. Suddenly Mrs. Soren looked up and yelled, "Look!"

Everyone's gaze focused on the kitchen counter at the other end of the room. There, strutting toward the uncarved rest of the turkey, was Chiro. Aaron grabbed his digital camera for a photo.

Catharine jumped up and sped toward Chiro. He took off. Everyone laughed. They would remember it forever.

On Friday afternoon, Rose Lauver's two sons helped their mother move into the farmhouse. They arrived around two o'clock in the afternoon with their version of the ubiquitous four-wheel drive pickup truck, this one dark blue. Rose drove her silver Corolla in behind them. A large, middle-aged woman with rosy cheeks in a round face, she wore the traditional prayer cap of the Mennonites; a long, navy wool skirt; a blue, long-sleeved blouse; a white apron; and comfortable black shoes.

"Hello," she said and introduced her "boys." "They came all the way from the other side of Snyder County to help. I'm sorry we're a bit late."

Catharine had cleaned Rose's room thoroughly, removed nonessentials, and put pale green linens on the four-poster bed dominating the room. A new puffy, white quilt and rose incense made the room feel fresh. A vase of silk red roses added color.

The farmhouse was a family museum going back to the 1800s. Rose's room had served as a master bedroom for generations of Weavers. A couple of dark-wood stands were original; one held a large, white basin and pitcher from the era. The room's expansive, many-paned windows overlooked the backyard and the fields and hills beyond. Rose's room, a bath, and her mother's room, took up the right side of the downstairs, with Rose located across the hall from the oblong kitchen and dining room.

Catharine's mother's room had once served as extra living space for the large families once residing at Jacob's Farm. Its windows opened on the porch, the front yard, and the entrance. An electric heater stood in the middle of an ancient stone fireplace for added heat. The room smelled of her mother's lilac-scented body powder. On the other side of the hall sat the parlor and the room storing Catharine's boxes.

The second story had four bedrooms and a bath. Catharine's

bedroom sat at the top of the stairs, decorated in her favorite shades of blue and yellow, and furnished with a familiar oak bureau and her grandmother's large maple chest, where she'd once displayed thirty dolls in international dress. An adjoining guest room stayed open; the others remained closed and empty except for two twin beds and Catharine's ginger couch, which kind neighbors had hauled up with great effort.

December 1 dawned sunny and a little less chilly. Chiro stayed at the farmhouse and curled up asleep next to Barney as they left in Aaron's packed truck. Though less complicated than the first move, this one had its down moments: Logan came along. Catharine stayed out of the way until Logan was sufficiently calmed and tied to a tree in the yard. This step didn't stop him from grabbing at a dress when she walked too closely while carrying a load of clothes on hangers. The dress fell to the ground and was torn between Logan's incisors before anyone could stop him.

"Logan," yelled Aaron as he put down a box and went after the dog. "No!"

Logan stopped immediately, the flowered housedress hanging from his mouth like a multicolored tongue.

Aaron gently took it from him and held it up for inspection. It was torn down one side; Catharine looked at it in disbelief. After a period of silence, she laughed. "Here we go again. Do you think Logan and I will ever get along?"

Aaron walked over and gave her a hug. "What can I say? I'm sorry, again."

"I never liked the dress anyway," she said.

CHAPTER 12

During the Christmas season, students gifted the community with music and drama. Aaron, Catharine, and her mother attended four programs, and Rose joined them for two concerts. Rose was an excellent caregiver, and Catharine's mother liked her.

A month earlier Catharine had purchased plane tickets to visit Matt and Carolyn in California for the two-week holiday break. She called them weekly and knew her grandchild was due anytime. She hoped the baby would be born during her stay.

She was, and they named the baby girl Sydney. This dark-haired cherubic bundle brought her great joy. She felt sad only because she wouldn't be there to see her grow.

Returning to Harrisburg, she anticipated seeing Aaron again. When Catharine saw him waiting at the airport, she ran into his open arms. He gave her a tight hug but only a casual kiss on her cheek. She had missed him, but was he holding back?

"I'm a grandmother now!" Catharine said. "Do I look different?"

"You're lit up like a Christmas tree. I don't think I have ever seen you so ebullient."

"Ebullient? Have you been working on your vocabulary?"

"I'm getting into your territory, since you mock my science terms."

They went directly to Jacob's Farm, where Catharine showed a plethora of baby and family photos from her camera and gave her mother a few she had printed.

"Mama, you're a great-grandmother!"

Then she hesitated. She had forgotten Sarah's son, George, and his children, as if they weren't part of the family—it had been a long time. She added, "I mean, again."

Her mother caught the significance of the remark, saying, "I know. They've forgotten us, haven't they?"

◈

Catharine left her car at the farm and rode back to the cottage with Aaron.

Classes started again the next morning but not for long.

On Thursday morning, freezing rain mixed with snow made the roads hazardous and walking dangerous; classes were canceled. Pine and spruce tree branches stood encased in ice, pointing to the ground like daggers. All afternoon Catharine heard crackling in the pine forest behind the house as wind blew through the trees. Periodically a thud reported the demise of another pine too old and fragile to stand any longer, like people when they reached the end of their days. She thought about her mother.

On Friday a horrific blizzard came howling down the valley, covering everything in a white, heavy, and wet blanket. When the wind stopped, she went outside. The snow muffled all sound and was as white and pure as the silence. Snow stuck to bushes looked like lace trimming.

Before noon the weather knocked out electricity in the area.

Catharine wouldn't go home this weekend. She didn't even have her car, since Aaron had driven her to the cottage Sunday evening.

She would call her mother on the cell phone if it could get through. Fortunately, about five years ago, Josie's husband had persuaded her mother to have Jerry purchase and install a generator at the farmhouse. Before the blackout, Rose called to say she would stay the weekend and not to worry.

In October, Aaron had demanded she arrange for plenty of logs for the wood stove. But then he went ahead and chopped up pieces from deadwood in the forest and stored them under the carport.

By the time he trudged through the snow to check on her Friday evening, she had a substantial amount of wood stacked on the brick hearth and the stove fired up.

"Hey, you do know how to build a fire," he said.

"Of course. I grew up in the country, remember?"

Catharine fixed hot chocolate from water boiled on the wood stove. The smell of chocolate mixed with the burning candles and smoke from the wood stove made her sleepy but cozy as she sank into the overstuffed couch. For the first time, they were alone at the cottage, relaxing and taking time to talk. Her heart beat a little faster as they sat close in the dim light. But Catharine made up her mind not to allow physical attraction to take over. It was too soon.

They talked in personal terms about their past and families.

"You know a lot about my family," said Catharine. "Tell me about your life; I know you are from the coal country in northern Pennsylvania."

"Okay, I will. As teenagers, my father and mother came with their parents from Poland and met over here. My mother was Jewish and my father Polish Catholic. Just like his father, he went to work in the mines after getting married."

Catharine perked up. "So you're Jewish, and it needs to be through your mother. How come you've never mentioned it, since I'm a Hebrew scholar and love everything Jewish?"

"I will remind you of that comment," he said.

Catharine felt her face flush and was glad for the darkness. "Did they keep the Jewish traditions?"

"No, my mother's family converted—well, *converted* isn't the right word. They felt forced to change from Judaism to Catholicism to get out of Poland and escape the Nazis. They left brothers and sisters and parents who never made it through the war. My brother didn't know their story until years later. Then he remembered that a lot of our meals consisted of traditional Jewish foods. By the time I was born, they could talk about it."

"You said your parents have died. What happened to them?"

"My father and grandfather both suffered black lung disease from working in the coal mines. My mother died of complications from diabetes and pneumonia about ten years ago."

"And your brother retired to Costa Rico? How old is he?"

"Stanislaus is twenty years my senior. He would now be seventy-three. I haven't seen him since our mother's funeral. He married a native girl and has a daughter. Every year they send a Christmas letter."

"And your boys—Keith and Loren? Do you ever see them?"

"Once in a while, one of them will come east. Mary took them to her family in California at the time of our divorce, fearful I would claim them. At first, I visited them a couple of times a year. Now they've left home; they come here. Their mother's remarried, and Keith is married and has a little girl. I went to his wedding but didn't feel comfortable with Mary's family. Maybe they felt sorry for me because she left 'to fulfill her life.' I give her credit—she's never bad-mouthed me to her family or the boys."

"And what about Loren?"

"He's still single and is a male nurse. He's traveled around the world alone and lived in Spain a couple of years where he learned Spanish and went to nursing school. He met a girl, but it didn't work out, so he finished nursing school in California and works in a hospital in San Diego. Being bilingual has helped his career."

"It sounds like you need to get back with your kids a little more."

Aaron didn't reply, but his head dropped.

"You must miss them, and you must have been lonely here without them."

"Sometimes, but I love the outdoors, hiking, and fishing. I wouldn't want to change it."

"It isn't much of a social life. How many single teachers are there?"

"There are six—two men and four career women. I have gone out to dinner with the two younger women. We're friends, but nothing ever clicked. Then you came along, and my life has been clicking ever since," he said, laughing.

"You mean a lot to me." He drew her close, and she laid her head on his shoulder. The room remained quiet as they watched bright-red flames jumping in every direction as if trying to escape through the stove's glass door.

The candles went out, and the only light came from the stove. Catharine fell asleep, comfortable, secure, and happy. Everything was wonderful—a professional was taking care of her mother, she liked her work, she felt secure with Aaron, and she was a grandmother. What could go wrong?

Around midnight she awoke as Aaron moved, jumped up, grabbed his flashlight, and rushed to the door. "What's wrong?" Catharine asked.

"I thought I heard someone trying to get in," he said.

He opened the door and stared into the night, shining the flashlight around the yard. Catharine came up and stood behind him. The light caught a dark figure clumsily running across the snow to an unseen vehicle. They heard the sound of a truck starting up, but no headlights came on as it moved away.

"Those look like footprints in the snow," she said.

"They most certainly are footprints."

Aaron got his coat on and went outside, shuffling through the snow. He came back in about ten minutes. "The footsteps went to the road. Whoever it was had a four-wheel drive vehicle, and they are long gone. I took photos of the prints with my digital camera.

"Since I walked over here and your car was gone, they didn't think anyone was home. I was asleep and didn't get up right away. They weren't just trying the door. It was more like trying to unlock it with something metal. Then they saw my flashlight. I think they planned to burglarize the place."

CHAPTER 13

"I scared him away," said Aaron. "I'm sure he won't be back tonight. If it's all right with you, I think I'll walk home. Logan needs feeding, and I shouldn't be seen coming home in the morning, should I? I'll call Zeph tomorrow."

"No problem. You're right, of course. I'm doing okay, and I'm not afraid." Catharine amazed herself at her lack of concern over the incident.

It wasn't a long walk across campus. Aaron's small house belonged to a complex of a dozen homes built for married students returning to college after World War II. They were located behind the men's dormitory, well maintained over the years and inexpensive; married students still rented them.

The next morning more snow covered the tracks of the mysterious night visitor. Catharine didn't go to church or leave the cottage. She could add nothing to a call from the sheriff other than assure him she was fine. She lay with Chiro, wrapped in a warm, thick comforter in front of the wood stove, and read by the light from the windows. The electric came on at about four o'clock in the afternoon, and she wrote in her devotional journal for the day.

Having lived in California for so many years, it's difficult for me to like winter. Nature has lost her charm and retreated into chilled indifference. I saw a thin doe rummage through a bare cornfield last week. Tiny birds huddle around their day's ration of seeds on the cleared walkway outside my door, all fluffed up as snowflakes pelt them and melt into their feathers. Winter means icy roads and lost work and news headlines chilling our psyche with "arctic cold seen on heels of new snow." It's a time when social life is restricted, and invitations must be prefaced with "if the roads aren't bad," and we're stuck in our stuffy houses for days. Beauty stepped back when the green valley went brown. But the quilt of snow now hiding it does have its own eye appeal. Down through the ages, the saints have always likened it to the robe of Christ's righteousness hiding our ugly sinfulness and forgiving us. Under the snowy robe, His Spirit lives in us just like the plants are protected until spring.

We live in the winter of the world, and it's hard to see God. We search for any sign of the end of winter and the recreation of the new earth and the spring of the world. Jesus will come, and like blossoms in the spring, the righteous of all ages shall burst from the earth. We have this hope.

The next week classes met in spite of the frigid weather. After her last class on Wednesday, Catharine made her daily call to the farm. No one answered. A few minutes later, her cell phone rang.

Rose's alarmed voice said, "I'm afraid there's been an accident, and your mother fell. I've called an ambulance, and they're on the way."

"Is she conscious? How bad is she?"

"She can't get up. She is in pain around her hip but conscious. Can you get here right away?"

"I will somehow. I left my car at the farm. I'll need to find Aaron and have him drive me there. Maybe I should meet you at the hospital. How are the roads?"

"Okay. Meet me in Lewistown. An ambulance can get up here with four-wheel drive, and they've cleared Thirty-Five and certainly the main route to Lewistown, so you can make it. I must go." And she hung up.

Catharine ran to find Aaron, and fortunately he hadn't left. "Can you take me to the Lewistown Hospital right away? My mother's fallen."

Aaron's four-wheel drive truck made the trip easily, bouncing over icy bumps even on the main road. The ambulance had arrived at the ER, and her mother lay in a bed behind one of the curtained areas, waiting for x-rays and tests. It would be a long wait, and she told Aaron to leave her there. Her mother would obviously be admitted to the hospital.

"I'll call you when I need a ride home," she said. His embrace calmed her, and he left.

By the time evening came, her mother was ensconced in a hospital bed. X-rays showed her hip wasn't broken, and she didn't need surgery. The fall had caused a fractured pelvis and would need initial care in the hospital, then rehab.

Catharine and Rose talked privately after the doctors gave the diagnosis.

Rose admitted to being out of the house at the time of the fall.

"I needed to check on my parents to see how they were doing and to get some things at the store," she told Catharine. "I'm so sorry, but I couldn't have been gone more than two hours."

Catharine got further confirmation from the ER doctor her mother would be in the hospital for a week and in rehab for at least a month. She discussed the situation with Rose.

Rose sat quietly—too quietly, she thought. Avoiding Catharine's eyes, she stared at the floor.

"What can you do while Mama is healing? Will you stay at the house?"

Rose raised her head and pursed her lips. "I'm sorry. I need to have an income, and I've been offered another job."

"What?" Catharine widened her eyes. "Already? Did you just call somebody?"

"No, I got the offer two days ago. It's to be in a private house close to Lewistown and stores. Catharine, your mother's house is just too remote. I was going to tell you, even if this hadn't happened. I didn't feel safe there."

"Why?"

"I'm not sure when it started—maybe a week ago, but I kept seeing a black van hanging around. They actually drove up the lane a couple times, and I think I heard someone in the yard more than once. I also saw a car coming up here at night, turning around, and leaving. I don't know what it looked like."

Catharine surmised that the car was the police stakeout Zeph had promised. She silently chastised herself for not telling Rose about it. But the van was another issue.

Rose continued, "I'm sure there was someone or something in the house two days ago. I've been too scared to sleep since."

"And you didn't tell me?"

"I guess I should have."

Catharine decided she was going to confront Ralph Brown on her own.

CHAPTER 14

Catharine headed straight from her last class to visit her mother at the hospital. She found her in surprisingly good spirits, propped up in bed with the tray in front of her holding her large-print Bible and Sabbath school lesson. She chuckled and said, "Well, I did myself up good this time, didn't I? I wasn't watchin' and stepped on Barney's tail."

"At least he didn't wind up in the hospital," said Catharine.

She continued, "Where is that niece and nephew of yours? They said they'd stop by."

As if on cue, Debbie swung into the room, her long, straight, light-brown hair half over her face. "How ya doin', Aunt Liz?" she said.

Aunt Liz responded with a smile, spreading her lips into a thin line.

"Come 'n' give me a real smile." Debbie swooped down on her great-aunt with an all-encompassing hug and planted a kiss on one of her gaunt cheeks.

The elderly woman grimaced. "My shoulder!" she said.

Debbie plopped down on the bed.

"Debbie, the beds aren't for sitting. You could spread germs," Catharine said.

Debbie jumped up and stood against the wall with one boot behind her and against it. Her dark-blue jeans clung tightly to her shapely legs.

"We can't stay long. We're on the way to pick up the kids from school," she said.

"Hey." Jerry tromped in, wearing his cowboy boots, jeans, and brown leather jacket. His blond hair stuck out in all directions from under his farm cap. He gave both older women brief hugs. A sweaty odor bounced off him to Catharine's nose. He took off the brown jacket and threw it in a corner. "Man, it's hot in here."

The couple drilled their aunt on her day and scolded her for not eating her green beans. "But they're so stringy," the woman whined. "I just fill up so fast, yet they tell me to keep eatin'."

Running out of questions, the pair reported on their kids and their aunt's cat, Barney. "That dern cat spit at me this morning," Jerry said. "And he pawed at me with those dragon claws. It was all I could do to get away from him. What nerve that animal has when I've been feedin' him." But he said this with a twinkle in his eye.

"He doesn't bother me," said Debbie. "He likes women better than men."

"So do I," Jerry responded.

The two of them spent the next five minutes bantering with each other as if they were the only people in the room. Debbie cocked her head and fondled the rings in her pierced ears. She tossed her long hair back when it fell into her line of vision, which happened every time she moved. Then, as if suddenly remembering that others were in the room, the two turned back to Catharine. Jerry asked how she was doing, but his tone lacked interest.

Catharine nodded and said, "I'm doing fine and enjoying my classes."

"I can't imagine anyone enjoying Hebrew. It looks like Chinese to me. I never got much out of Bible study at the Mennonite school. I guess I'm just not intellectual," he said, enunciating the last word.

"We all have different interests," said Catharine. "I wouldn't make a good farmer."

"Well, we'd better be on our way," said Jerry, picking up his jacket from the floor. After giving the two women brief hugs, they disappeared around the corner.

Catharine let a period of silence go by and then commented that they seemed like busy people.

Her mother's mood rallied after their visit. Catharine didn't want to change the atmosphere, so they watched television together for the next hour.

✆

Almost from the beginning of her church membership transfer to Mifflintown, Catharine taught Sabbath school two out of four weeks of the month. She alternated with an overworked public school teacher, who did more than his share of sermons and other duties.

In mid-December she received a call from the pastor, Jonathan Allen.

Pastor Jon said, "I have a favor to ask of you. We are privileged to have a real theologian at our little church, and we would like to use you as much as we can. The board is wondering if you have the time to teach a Bible study during the week."

He continued, "It's been a long time since this little church had regular Wednesday prayer meetings. The membership is spread all over the county. So we wanted something for the members and closer community. We felt a Bible study along the lines of what you already teach would be great. Are you interested?"

"Yes, I see the possibilities," Catharine said. "Wouldn't Wednesdays compete with other churches having Wednesday night meetings?"

"We thought of that, so we decided on Thursdays for the Bible study. I think it could appeal to the community, and I want to advertise it. I belong to the local ministerial association, and I would tell them about it. As a teacher at the college, you won't carry the stigma of being denominational."

It seemed like a reasonable request, for which she already had material, so Catharine agreed. When she told Aaron about the studies, his response surprised her.

"Do you really think you'll have time for it, with visiting your mother, keeping up your exercise program, and doing other projects? Didn't you also restart their community services food and clothing program?"

Catharine's first thought was, *Is he telling me what to do?* And some rebellious thoughts surfaced. But she remembered that with ADD, a person had to force herself to rein in her enthusiasm. She saw life as filled with so many interesting things to do and hated to miss any of them. In the end, she ignored his advice.

Aaron's next response surprised her even more. "If you really plan to get involved with this, am I invited too?"

"Of course, Aaron. I would be pleased to have you there."

The Thursday class began in mid-January.

She didn't invite her students to the church group—it didn't seem appropriate in the diverse campus setting. However, it wasn't long before one of the Iraq war veterans saw the notice in the local paper and started coming. The word spread, and at least five more students and the vet's wife attended. She was glad to have the students show up in spite of the weather. The senior church members didn't usually attend if it rained or snowed. A few people from the community also attended.

Aaron came when he could spare time from classwork. Their differences in religious outlook bothered Catharine as she saw their relationship grow. She looked forward to seeing him and hearing from him. To invite himself to the Bible study, she thought, affirmed that he felt the same.

His decision made her happy, because she thought he'd lost interest in church. In spite of teaching at a Bible college, he didn't attend any church in the area. The campus church was the only one he went to on occasion; they had gone there together a couple of times.

At the end of November, Aaron called on a Friday. "Why don't I go to church with you tomorrow?"

He attended three times. The third time the pastor presented a sermon on the book of Revelation and inferred that the Roman church system could be the Beast of Revelation and described the atrocities organized religion had carried out over the centuries. The Reformation, he said, began a new day, but even those churches could become an image to the Beast in the last days if they all joined together in a state religion.

Aaron didn't say much on the way home. Catharine felt uncomfortable and finally asked what he thought of it.

"Well, it doesn't help win friends among other Christians," he said. "He reflects Luther's belief about Rome, and the Inquisition and religious crime are historically correct, but even the Reformation brought out zealots who persecuted Catholics and other Christians. Think about your Mennonite ancestors. Didn't you say one of them was drowned in Switzerland by Zwinglians because of his belief about baptism?"

"Yes, that's true," Catharine said. "The Mennonites and Amish have never persecuted any one. They are pacifists. So is my church. I think it's why my father joined them—they still had the reputation of people of peace and added a few other concepts like rejecting the eternal hellfire and damnation motif. He hated that."

"And well he should have," Aaron said.

"But labeling all post-Constantine Christians as apostate is overdoing it. We know Hitler was German and killed six million of my people, yet we don't distrust Germans today."

"I know, and I don't distrust other Christians. It's a political religious system uniting with government that's caused persecution in the past. Today we see it in the Middle East. Sure, we have a few differences in Bible interpretation, but none of them are on the divinity of Christ and His sacrifice for us."

As he parked the car, Aaron turned to Catharine. She felt him looking deep into her eyes—or was it her soul?—and asking sincerely, "If I don't buy into all your church teaches, would you still like me?"

Lying abed later, Catharine could think of nothing else: Aaron's soulful inquiry as if his value to her depended on his accepting her religion. She wondered, *How many seekers of truth feel put in such a position? It wasn't just my church but all evangelicals. Do Christians approach people with the invitation to accept Christ with strings attached? Do they cause friends or family to feel rejected if they don't respond positively to the formula offered them? How could you relate to someone who felt you were lost if you didn't embrace his or her belief system? Was it any wonder many rejected it?*

CHAPTER 15

After ten days in the hospital, an ambulance took Catharine's mother to Eden Court, an assisted-living home closer to the southern part of the county.

During the second week of Mama's rehab at Eden Court, Catharine scheduled an appointment with Lisa Connelly, her social worker.

When she saw her mother after the appointment, she was sitting in the forest-green La-Z-Boy recliner under the window. Catharine hugged her; her mother didn't respond with her usual half smile. Her mother's lined face lacked her traditional rosy glow. *Will it ever come back?* Over the years her once-green eyes had paled; her auburn hair had become dull and thin but not gray. Today she looked her age.

"Mama, I've just been talking to Mrs. Connelly," Catharine said cautiously.

"Oh?" Mama's thin, pale lips opened and formed the word slowly. She looked at her daughter out of the corner of her eye. Turning her head would be painful, but the look came across to Catharine as one of suspicion.

"Do you like it here any better today? What did you have for lunch?"

The older woman latched onto the lunch question and described in detail what she'd eaten. "How I wish I could eat like I used to. It just didn't taste good, but I did good."

Catharine knew better, for the nurse had said she'd eaten very little.

"How did the day go?" she repeated.

Her mother looked downcast. "I just wanna go home."

"You know, Mama, it's not possible. There's no one to be with you full-time with Rose out of the picture, and if we got professional help from outside the area, it would cost more than Eden Court."

"I just want to take care of myself!" she said with more energy than previously expressed. "There's Jerry and Debbie. They come by a lot. Maybe, maybe they'll come live with me."

"No, Mama. They have two young children. They have too much on their plate now." *And they don't need a disabled person to care for*, she thought.

A wave of despair flooded over Catharine. She felt her eyes tearing. She thought of the empty farmhouse without Mama; she remembered the empty town house without Kenji—the feelings. They seemed so much alike.

Jacob's Farm, a place called home, a part of family life for decades. At Christmas or in summer, they came back to be with Mama or "Grandma." Without Mama, the house was just an old building, like a lifeless body. In an automatic gesture of helplessness, she turned her hands out and up, and slammed them down on her lap.

Catharine said, "I'm sorry my work is so far from the farm, but now it's closer than it used to be. I can come here, not just on weekends, but during the week at least once. I'll still call every day."

Her mother's face contorted, and she sobbed; the sobs became more intense until they made her cough. Catharine rose and held on to her. Between sobs, she choked out in hoarse whispers, "I'm just an old lady nobody has time for. I don't wanna be a burden to anybody."

"No, no," Catharine whispered back. A long silence ensued as they held each other.

Every time she broached the idea of staying at Eden Court, her mother stubbornly rejected it. Now the decision to stay had to be finalized. The house wasn't safe for two reasons: her mother being alone and the threat she couldn't disclose.

Catharine reminded her of the fall and when Rose took her to the hospital for being disoriented. "Remember, you couldn't remember?" she said as if talking to a child.

Her mother nodded. "But I can now."

Mama's bouts with memory loss came and went, but Catharine knew she covered them up by saying yes when she was confused. She'd gotten a call from the night nurse at Eden Court last week, saying Mama had gone to the lobby door in the middle of the night. She'd tried to unlock it and called for Catharine.

Her mother looked glum. Catharine could understand. She knew what being left alone felt like and recognized the crunch of time. To be ninety-three and forced out of familiar surroundings would be much worse. Looking over her mother's head through the window, she noticed two large ravens sitting on snow-covered tree limbs. Ordinarily she would have been excited to see them so close, but today they looked menacing, even ominous, like dark wraiths that had come to torture her. She glared at them silently for several minutes.

Catharine heard a soft knock on the door. She turned, and the birds flew away.

"Come in," she said.

Mrs. Connelly entered the room. She made an imposing figure: tall, fortyish, dressed in a sterile-looking, white pantsuit. Her straight blonde hair sat on her head like a helmet. Unlike her intimidating appearance, her voice was calm, soft, and warm. Words oozed out of her mouth gradually with the kind of assurance sick people need. "Is everything okay?" she asked.

Under the gaze of her social worker, Mama dried her eyes. Then she perked up and turned to Mrs. Connelly. "Yes," she said, as if nothing had happened.

"I need to check your medical records with you and your daughter." She took a folding chair from the closet, sat down, and opened a thick, brown file folder. In the next few minutes, she went over the reports and asked questions. After a brief discussion, Mrs. Connelly stated firmly, "In my opinion you cannot go home this winter. It will be too dangerous for you to live alone. You are so far out in the country. It wouldn't be safe, even if you had someone living with you."

There it was—out in the open.

"No, no." Her mother grimaced and put her head down in her hands.

Mrs. Connelly gently stroked her back. "That's okay. I know this is hard for you."

"Why do you say I can't go home?" Mama mumbled.

Mrs. Connelly reminded her of the fall in her home and her episode of being disoriented.

"Yes, but it went away." She seemed to be pleading now.

Mrs. Connelly reminded her of the night she went to the lobby door at Eden Court, saying Catharine was calling her. "Think if you had been at home. You could have sleepwalked into the frigid cold, fallen, and died of hyperthermia. Now, Elizabeth, tell me what you don't like about being here."

The ninety-three-year-old adjusted her gold-rimmed, thick glasses and moved her body around until her eyes focused on a dust ball in one corner. Catharine noticed it had been there for days.

Turning stiffly, she inspected the room again. "I really don't like the color, and the shades don't get pulled down every night. And they get me up too early, and breakfast isn't served till a lot later. My daughter could tell you more. She could make a list of stuff."

Through the rest of Mrs. Connelly's explanation of how some of these things could be changed, Mama sat downcast and still, looking at the patternless, worn brown carpet beneath her varicose-blue feet.

Catharine listened. *It doesn't sound as if Mama is going to be happy here.*

CHAPTER 16

This was the day for unfinished business. Catharine thought it was time to meet Ralph Brown. The sun shone in an azure sky. It was a Sunday between the snowstorms rolling through the valley, one after another, with a day or two in between. Her mother's situation and the storms had held up her determination to confront him.

She had found the address, just outside Lewistown, in Kenji's journal. According to Sheriff Zeph, the Brown family still lived in the same house, and he was ready to pick up Ralph at any time she noticed another mysterious stalker. Catharine didn't want him to do this, believing Ralph was just a kid acting on the wrong information.

She left the cottage around ten and drove west toward Lewistown, following directions copied from online. When she found the house, shock caused her to sit in the car while taking in the disturbing scene. A once-beautiful three-story Victorian home sat like an elegant old woman wearing worn-out, tattered garments. Paint peeled from its sides and the balcony's broken railing, making it look as if it hadn't been touched since Edmond Brown fell from it forty years ago. The wraparound front porch's ornate pillars stood chipped and gray. The steep-pitched roof, with weathered red-and-white trim, looked sad and in need of repair. Fallen tree branches lay like dark bones strewn across the yard's covering of white snow.

It took Catharine several minutes to get the courage to go to the door. She wished she'd told Aaron what she was doing, but she was afraid he wouldn't approve. She thought having a man present might intimidate young Ralph.

A woman, looking as disheveled as the house, answered the doorbell. She appeared fiftyish, with short graying hair. She wore a T-shirt and too-tight jeans over her oversized body.

"Mrs. Brown?"

"Yes, I'm Marvina Brown."

"My name is Catharine. I live over in Juniata County. Is your son, Ralph, at home?"

"He's upstairs. What has he done now?"

"I don't know if he has done anything, but I am following up on a letter I think he sent me when I started teaching at Midland Bible College. It was left on my desk. I'm afraid it's a little threatening."

"Why would my son threaten you?" Her voice sounded hostile and incredulous.

"Apparently he may have gotten some wrong information about what happened here more than forty years ago. My name is Catharine Yamashiro, and my husband once lived in this house when he came from Japan."

"Come in," she said, finally opening the door and bringing Catharine into the warmth of the house. The woman showed her a seat in a large, partially furnished living room. "You mean, the student my father-in-law brought here from Japan to help us, the one who ran away? Where is he now?"

Catharine said, "He had to leave, but it's another story unrelated to this. My husband died two years ago, but I have come back to teach at the Midland Bible College and be near my mother. But right now I must ask Ralph if he wrote this letter and why." She held out the unfolded yellow sheet.

"Ralph, come down here," his mother yelled up the winding stairs near the entrance.

Hurried footsteps echoed on the stairs, and a young man appeared. Catharine thought he was rather nice looking, with a blond crew cut and a good build, but he was older than a kid.

"Ralph, I am Catharine Yamashiro, and I think you may have left a note on my desk at Midland Bible College about a month ago. Did you do this?" She spoke without tones of accusation or anger and showed him the note.

Ralph's blue eyes widened, and he stared at her as if in disbelief that she had come to see him. "He killed my grandfather, and I have to revenge his death somehow."

"Who told you that? Your father?"

"No."

Catharine turned to Mrs. Brown. "Do you know anything about it? Where is your husband? I understand he was there."

"My husband, Joe, died more than ten years ago. Ralph is all I have now, and he's not well."

Catharine stared at the healthy young man standing before her but said nothing. "Where did you hear such a thing?" she said

"Someone called me on the phone and told me I had to revenge my grandfather's death."

"Who?"

"I don't know. They said it was God's will."

Mrs. Brown interrupted. "Mrs. Yamashiro, Ralph often hears voices. He has delusions. So if he wrote such a letter, he didn't mean it. He has never been violent like his father. He wouldn't hurt anyone."

"His father was violent? Did he have a mental disease?"

"No, he was just a violent drinker. I think something happened to him after his father's fall; at least that's what his mother said before she died."

Catharine felt compassion for the young man. "Do you take medication?"

"Mostly, when I remember it. But I'm tellin' the truth. Someone on the phone told me to write the letter and hang around your farm in Richfield."

Mrs. Brown looked at Catharine and shook her head. It was obvious she didn't believe her son.

"Do you mind if I talk to Ralph?" Catharine said.

"Go ahead, but please be nice, or he could get frightened and have a relapse."

"I understand. I'll be sympathetic."

As Catharine talked with Ralph, she found him to be an engaging young man who was occasionally plagued by voices and hallucinations. None of what he described sounded threatening. He also worked as a cashier at a nearby convenience store and drove the family van.

She explained to him the circumstances under which Edmond Brown had died as Marvina Brown listened intently. "Kenji wasn't anywhere near your grandfather when he fell. Do you understand and believe what I am telling you, Ralph?"

"I don't know. I guess. But who was on the phone?"

"I don't know. Was it a man's voice?"

"Yes. He had some kind of accent."

"Would you recognize his voice if you heard it again?"

"Maybe, I don't know." After a moment of silence, Ralph

said, "I'm sorry about the letter. I won't do it again or go to your farm."

"I forgive you, Ralph. I know you won't do me any harm." She gave him a hug. "I'm glad I met you, Ralph. You're a fine young man. Just be sure you keep taking your medicine regularly. Maybe we'll see each other again."

"I'll see you out," said Marvina.

As they stepped into the entrance area, Marvina lowered her voice and said, "Mrs. Yamashiro, I'm sure there was no phone call. Ralph probably had missed his medicine at the time. When I think about it, I believe my husband may have said once that your husband pushed his father. I didn't believe it, because the police would have found out, and my husband was a liar. One thing about Ralph—I don't think I've ever heard him tell a lie; it's not in him. Sometimes mentally ill people are more honest and real than the rest of us."

"You know, Marvina, I think you're right. And please call me Catharine. If there's any way I can be of help, please give me a call."

Catharine wrote her name and cell phone number on a piece of paper and gave it to Marvina. She didn't give her a card with her address at the cottage. She had no indication that Ralph knew she had moved, and this left some unanswered questions.

The two women hugged, and Catharine walked to her car.

CHAPTER 17

The next day dawned behind grayish-white, low-lying clouds as thick, falling snow threatened to close the college. It looked like another snowbound afternoon and a good time to make phone calls. First Catharine called Marvina Brown to see how Ralph was doing and whether he'd shown any aftereffects from their talk.

Marvina seemed grateful for Catharine's interest in him. "He's doing fine," she said, "actually less nervous."

"Forgiveness is healing."

"You know, dear, I heard that after your husband left here, he went to live with a farm family. Maybe you should talk to them about his stay in the area."

"That's what I plan to do today while the weather is too bad to go out."

She felt thankful for the woman's interest and cordiality, even surprised by them.

Marvina's encouragement to contact Kenji's foster parents pushed her to open the latest local telephone directory and look up all the Yoders in the county. A quick glance showed more than ten. But there was no Samuel or Rachel Yoder. She was sure of the names and wondered whether they had passed on. *But there should be a relative.* She began with the first—Abraham Yoder—and punched in his number.

"Hello, is this the Abraham Yoder residence?"

"Ja," an elderly male voice answered.

"My name is Catharine Yamashiro, and I am trying to find some friends of my husband when he lived here. Do you know Samuel and Rachel Yoder?"

"Not for some three years. Haven't seen 'em. They're my third cousins. The last I heard, they was in a nursing home in McAlisterville."

"Could you tell me the name of the nursing home? Are they able to have visitors?"

"I dunno. Let me ask Ruth if she knows. Ruth, da ya remember the name of that place in McAlisterville, where Sam and Rach went to live?"

A woman's voice from the background said, "I think it was McAlisterville Nursing Home."

"McAlisterville Nursing Home," Abraham reported so loudly that Catharine jerked the phone away from her ear.

"Do you know how they are doing? Could they have visitors?"

"I really dunna know. What if I get ya their daughter's name and ya can talk to her? We don't get around much now, what with Ruth's arthritis and such."

"I'm sorry. Yes, please."

"That's Anna Yoder, and her husband's Cecil Yoder. They're in the phone book and live in McAlisterville. Sam and Rach lived with them till Sam got outta his mind, and Rach couldn'a stand to be separated from him, so they both went to the nursing home."

"Why does Cecil have the Yoder name?"

"That's the name of half the county." He chuckled. "Nah, they're not related."

"Thank you. I see a Cecil Yoder in the phone book. I appreciate your help. Good-bye."

"Bye."

Catharine punched in Cecil Yoder's number. A woman answered. "Hello?"

"Hello, is this Anna Yoder?"

"Yes" The voice sounded like a middle-aged woman.

"My name is Catharine Yamashiro, the wife of Kenji. I'm trying to contact his foster parents from the late 1960s, Samuel and Rachel Yoder. I understand you are their daughter."

There was a long silence before the voice on the phone said hesitantly, "I see. Why do ya want to see them?"

"Well, I thought they would like to know what happened to Kenji over the years and know he died two years ago."

"Oh. I'm sorry your husband died, Mrs. Yamashiro, but talkin' about him would only make my mother unhappy. My father has dementia, and we are glad he can't remember him."

"What? Why do you say 'glad'? Didn't he like him?"

"He loved him like a son, but you know what I mean, don't ya—after what happened."

"I don't know what you are talking about. What happened?" Catharine felt her body go limp as a feeling of unreality set in.

"You don' know? He never told ya?" She sounded amazed and continued, "Maybe I'd better talk to ya straight." She said this softly, her voice no longer threatening, almost sympathetic. "I'll tell ya where we live, so stop by one evenin' when my husband's home. I need to start his supper now."

"Yes, of course I will, but with all this snow, I'm not sure when. Where do you live?"

"Our farm's near Evandale, a white farmhouse off Shade Road, across from a bunch of houses. We have a long lane. Look for a big silo nearby and lotsa gray buildings. Yoder is on the white mailbox at da front."

"Thank you, Mrs. Yoder. I will call first."

"That'll be good."

Catharine hung up the phone, unaware of anything but what she had just heard. What awful thing had her husband done to hurt the Yoders?

CHAPTER 18

With this latest jarring news, Catharine felt her life falling apart. After one enigma connected with her husband had been mostly resolved, another had risen. This was worse than being threatened; it struck like an ax at the root of their happy marriage. He had secrets he hadn't shared with her. Now, when she wanted to move on, they floated over her sunny sky like dark clouds. The clouds contained a rail ticket across Canada, an unopened letter, missing journal pages, stalkers, mystery vehicles, and an ethereal phone call to a mentally ill young man, telling him to kill her.

Aaron tended to brush off unusual happenings with practical explanations. Maybe he could put her mind at ease now. When she called him, he insisted on walking over through the snow.

"So what's going on, Cat? You sound troubled."

"Sit down. I'll try to start from the beginning."

"More than two years ago, Kenji gave me an unopened letter to keep. He said if something happened to him, I should give it to a lawyer named Miles Pollack. He said to wait two years until the politics changed where he worked."

She continued, "But just before I moved up here, I read Miles Pollack had died of a heart attack at his home in Bethesda."

"You still have the letter?"

"Yes, but I can't find it; I don't remember where I put it when I packed all my stuff to come up here. Then this threat came with the note on my desk followed by the apparent stalking and someone trying to get in here."

"You mean Ralph Brown?"

"I'm not sure. I went to confront him the other day."

"You what? How could you do such a foolish thing by yourself?"

"I was afraid you wouldn't approve or that you would intimidate the boy if you went with me."

"I certainly wouldn't have approved; it was dangerous. What happened?"

"He lives with his mother, and they were both very nice. I think they are poor, as the house isn't kept up."

"Forget the house. What did he say?"

"He admitted to the letter and said someone had called and told him to write it and take revenge for his grandfather's death because God wanted him to do it."

"That's crazy. Is he mentally ill?"

"He has a mental disease, but his mother says he is never violent. Yet he does hear voices when he isn't on his medication."

"Oh!" He shook his head and frowned. "Then that explains everything, and we can relax now and pray he stays on his medicine!"

"He really believes he got the call and says he hung around the farmhouse to scare me. I never told him I moved. It wasn't him trying to get in here when the lights went out."

"I wouldn't trust his beliefs if I were you."

"Now something else has happened." She closed her eyes and pushed her hair back. "I tried to find the people Kenji stayed with during his last year of high school and while he worked. They are in a rest home, but their daughter says they won't see me because of something Kenji did. She said to come and talk to her about it." Catharine started to cry as Aaron hugged her.

"When do you want to see them? I'll go with you."

"Maybe you shouldn't. It might put them off seeing me with another man after only two years."

She knew she had said the wrong thing when he stepped back and gave her a long, pained look.

"Are you saying we shouldn't be seeing each other because Kenji died two years ago? I thought we had more going for us." He turned away.

"No, I meant in this culture …"

"You still talk about him a lot; you haven't moved on." He turned and stared out the window. "I'm competing with a ghost!"

"No, no, there is no competition!"

"Anyway." He lowered his voice and took a deep breath. "We haven't talked about the future, I shouldn't assume anything. You're right. You need to go see them alone. I'd better go now." And he left.

Catharine sat there, shocked. She thought over the conversation and teared up. Chiro came from some hidden place to comfort her and sat on her lap, nuzzling her face.

"My only friend here," she said. She wiped the water from her face and went to the fridge for frozen yogurt with fudge topping.

◆◆◆

She didn't see Aaron at the college the next day. After class she worked in her office and went to the gym for her running and weights routine. It was a welcome outlet for her emotions. In the evening, before her class at church, Aaron called and apologized. She also apologized; for what she wasn't sure, but it had to be an

ADD faux pas. *Has my determination to go alone to the Yoders put up a barrier, or is he too possessive?* The relationship made her feel overwhelmed. She didn't know what was appropriate in the modern dating game.

✒

On Friday after school, she visited her mother at Eden Court. She wanted to see her but dreaded the repeated questioning and whining to go home. Debbie and Jerry stopped by Eden Court frequently and checked the farmhouse every couple of days for signs of frozen pipes and other mishaps. They had taken Barney, Mama's yellow tabby, to their house.

Using her cell phone, Catharine called from the Eden Court lobby.

"Hello, Mrs. Yoder, this is Catharine Yamashiro. I'm out visiting my mother. Can I stop by your house in about thirty minutes?"

"Hello, ma'am. My husband's here. Sure, we can talk."

Shade Road was where her old friend, Janice, used to live. Her house now looked dark and empty. It hadn't been sold; maybe Janice would come back in the spring. She missed her, for they had stayed in contact over the years.

She saw the white mailbox with the Yoders' name on it and turned in.

At the house an attractive, wholesome-looking young Mennonite woman answered the door. She was Anna's daughter, Esther, one of Catharine's students in Bible history.

"Hello, Esther. I'm surprised and pleased to see you. How are you these cold days?"

"I'm great," she said, smiling. "I think you're here to see my mother. I'll call her."

Anna Yoder came from the kitchen, wearing an apron as pleasant dinner smells emanated through the door she had just opened.

"Have I come at an inconvenient time?" asked Catharine.

"Oh, no, Esther can carry on with supper. Let's go to the parlor."

Catharine sat on a couch with Anna across from her in an overstuffed chair. Unlike her daughter, she spoke with a Pennsylvania Dutch accent but chose her words carefully. She described the years when Kenji had lived like a brother in their house.

"There were seven of us—Kenji was the seventh: four boys and three girls. I was six years old, and my sisters were eight and sixteen. Mae was a year younger than Kenji. We played board games and softball games like most families. Being close in age, Mae and Kenji studied a lot together. He said she taught him English. But he was so smart; I doubt he needed much tutoring. He probably helped her through school more than she did him.

"When Kenji graduated from high school, he asked to stay here and pay rent, and my parents were more than glad to have him. They paid him for his farm labor, and he also had a job at a factory in Lewistown. He worked hard because he wanted to go to college. But clearly Mae adored him, and he cared for her. My father thought they spent too much time together, and after a year, he asked Kenji to leave. Kenji begged for his permission to marry her. My father told him how hard it would be for them to marry in this world—as it was then. They were of different races and religions. He totally objected to the latter, because we are Old Order Mennonites.

"My parents let Mae visit a girlfriend in Philadelphia for a week or two to get over it, and Kenji found a room in Lewistown.

"The day Mae was to come home, we got a call from Ellicott City, Maryland. They said they had gotten married and wanted our blessing. My father became enraged, and my mother cried. He called the police and reported her as missing. The police picked them up.

"Kenji was told to never come here again. They annulled the marriage, and to keep them apart, they sent Mae to an aunt and uncle in Canada. She never spoke to her parents again, nor did she come home. This happened years ago."

A long silence followed. Catharine felt dizzy and couldn't say anything. *Kenji had kept this to himself all these years.* She was stunned. Then she remembered something.

"Where in Canada did she go?"

"A small town near Edmonton, Alberta," Anna said.

Catharine felt like she had been knifed.

CHAPTER 19

Too stunned for tears, Catharine left the Yoders and backtracked to Jacob's Farm. The house looked forsaken and dark. Jerry's attempt to push snow from the road with the tractor had left the lane icy and dangerous. She drove up slowly, parked in front, and stepped in Jerry's footprints while going up the porch stairs. Once inside she went to the storage room. She needn't look far for the journal box; it was open. She didn't remember leaving it that way, but maybe she did. No, all the three remaining brown envelopes were gone. She remembered when Rose had hold told her she heard someone in the house.

Catharine scurried through the house, looking for any evidence of break-in, but she saw none. Then she quickly ran to the door and let herself out. Once in the car, she did some deep breathing for a few moments before starting it. When she did, the wheels churned without moving in the snow, making a loud grinding sound. It would soon be dark, and she felt frightened. She had put a bag of cat litter in the trunk, so she opened it and spread some under the back wheels. She tried once more to get out of the snowy rut before calling Jerry for help. Finally the car sped off at high speed over the dangerous road. When she realized what she was doing—trying to escape—she slowed down on Route 35 and went below the speed limit the rest of the way to the cottage.

Tempted to call Aaron, Catharine believed she had to calmly think this through on her own. She asked herself many questions over the next hour. *Did I really know Kenji Yamashiro after thirty years of marriage? Had he been involved in some clandestine project at work or even a romance with his high school sweetheart? What did the journals contain that someone didn't want me to see or needed for his or her own purposes? Was it connected with Mae Yoder in some way? Why else did he go to Edmonton without telling me? And what about the unopened envelope I can't find?*

Catharine was tired but not sleepy when Aaron called. "How did your visit go?"

"Horrible," she said. "I found out I'm a second wife!"

"You're kidding!"

Silence.

"You aren't kidding. It's almost midnight, but do you want me to come over?"

"No, we both have to be in class tomorrow. I'll see you before or after class. Come to my office. Thank you for being my friend through all of this," she said.

"Of course, you're my best friend."

"Thank you. Good night."

Catharine slept only five hours that night, a fitful, nightmarish sleep. After she awoke, she didn't feel like going through her regular devotional time and meditation. Her mind would wonder down all sorts of ugly paths if she tried.

After dressing and getting ready to go, Chiro, who usually sat with her during her meditation, seemed confused. He jumped on the couch in their regular place and began meowing loudly as he did when demanding food. But she had fed him. Finally she got the message. They shouldn't break protocol and skip communicating with Yeshua ("Jesus" in Hebrew) because of her feelings.

"Feelings can't be trusted," she said to Chiro. "Thank you, little friend." This time she put on her treasured Hebrew prayer shawl and sat still with head raised and prayed aloud to keep her mind from wandering.

Running late, Catharine called Aaron to come to her office after class.

When he arrived, she went over the conversation with Anna, then discussed the questions she had mulled over last night. "Concerning the Edmonton ticket," she asked, "how do you read that?"

"I can't conceive of Kenji carrying on a long-distance romance after thirty years of marriage to you. I'm sure there is another reason for the trip, maybe just business. Did he ever talk about trouble on the job?"

"Yes, in one area. The director, Dr. Raymond Kushner, calls himself an evangelical atheist. He went out of his way to taunt Kenji about his Christian faith and often said he belonged to the 'flat-earth society.' Kenji was their brightest physicist, but Kushner purposely undermined his work. Kenji looked forward to the time when Kushner would be retiring. It may be about now or soon."

"Tell me. Did Kenji believe in evolution?"

"I don't think so, at least not like most of them did. He believed in an old earth, like in Genesis 1:1, but with life much more recent—more than six thousand years—but not billions. He questioned some of the hypotheses on which scientists made decisions. Some of his colleagues, when faced with unanswerable questions, declared that life came with aliens from outer space or that the earth was seeded with microbes from an asteroid.

"Well, that wouldn't explain how life first came about out there either, but I understand; I have problems in this area myself, and I continue to teach at a fundamentalist college. I think I've shared these thoughts with you before. Getting back to our subject, I can't imagine an institution going after him now unless they suspected he had made some outstanding discovery in physics and are looking to steal it."

"A possibility, I suppose," said Catharine. "Unfortunately, I have to lead a Bible study at church tonight. I am so drained. I feel like calling it off, but I won't."

"You've had some shocks recently. What if I drive you? I promise not to embarrass you with questions. I'll just keep quiet."

"Sure."

Later, driving home from the church, they discussed the subject of the study, and his review of her teaching made Catharine feel affirmed.

When they arrived at the dark cottage, Catharine said, "I meant to leave the outside light on, but I guess I forgot—yes, I forgot it again. Now we'll need to walk carefully in the dark to avoid tripping."

The door opened easily—too easily. "It's not locked," she said.

"Don't go in," warned Aaron.

Aaron jumped forward and flipped the light switch to the right of the door.

A shocking scene lay before them. The cottage had been trashed. Drawers had been opened, their contents thrown on the floor. The couch had been turned over; the desk had been totally taken apart. Kitchen cupboards had been searched.

Catharine, her eyes wide and mouth open, screamed, "Where's Chiro?"

Aaron held her back as he went in first. "They were looking

for something and just waiting for you to leave some night. I'm calling the sheriff."

Catharine pushed him aside and ran through the house, calling for Chiro.

The bedroom was also in shambles, and the new mattress had been cut open. She found Chiro trembling in a corner of the closet.

CHAPTER 20

Aaron called the sheriff while Catharine waited with Chiro in her car. Zeph and two police cars from Mifflintown sped up the road thirty minutes later. With sirens turned off, they entered the campus, but anyone awake saw the flashing lights.

Zeph jumped out of the first car and informed her, "I've sent my other man to pick up Ralph for questioning."

"He didn't do it. You can't disturb him."

"How do you know he didn't do it?"

"Because I went to see him and his mother."

"You did what?"

"I went to confront him. He admitted that he wrote the letter, but he's never been here. It will only cause him harm if you bring him in."

"We already know he sent the note, but why would we harm him?" Zeph frowned.

"He has a mental illness."

"Oh, so we're dealing with a nut case." He threw up his arms. "Now I'm sure he did it."

"He said someone told him to send the note," Catharine said.

"A voice, I suppose?" Zeph said, sneering.

Catharine whispered, "Yes," and turned away.

Zeph and his men searched the cottage, while Catharine checked her desk. Except for a lone twenty-dollar bill for emergencies, she kept no cash in the house. The bill was gone.

"If they wanted money, they didn't make a big haul," she said. By this time, Catharine was beginning to see some humor in her situation. *Sometimes when one experiences enough "adventurous" events*, she thought, *he or she just has to laugh at them.* But she was still trembling.

Because it was late and she had classes in the morning, Catharine thought it best to stay at a motel in Mifflintown. She grabbed a few pieces of clothing and tossed them in a suitcase. She gently put Chiro in his cage, prepared a small cat box, and threw in a couple of cans of cat food.

"You need to go to a place where you can relax. What about the colonial bed-and-breakfast just down the road? They'll give you breakfast, and you'll have a beautiful room," Aaron said, stroking her hair.

"It's too late. I wouldn't disturb them at this hour."

"It's just nine thirty; I'll call. I know Verona and Bob Jenkins well. I stayed with them five years ago when I came here, and we've been good friends since. My kids stay there when they come to town."

"Okay, what about Chiro?"

"I'll tell them—not a problem, for you."

She held on to his arm, repeating, "Ralph didn't do this."

Aaron called Jenkins while they waited.

Having seen the police lights, Professor Koster and his wife came out of the estate house and walked down the drive to see what was going on. Catharine and Aaron told her about the robbery.

Catharine said, "We don't know if anything is missing yet."

"Then you must stay in my house tonight," Miriam said.

Catharine looked at Aaron. "We've made some other arrangements. Your place might be too close to the cottage for her to sleep. Not that you aren't safe; they're not coming back, I'm sure," he said.

To avoid any misunderstanding, Catharine added, "I've made arrangements to stay at the bed-and-breakfast down the road. But thank you anyway, Miriam."

Aaron drove her as they discussed the break-in. "They were looking for something. Do you have any idea what it could have been?"

"I don't know. I can only speculate that it has something to do with Kenji's work."

She reminded him of the mysterious missing letter. "I knew it was important, and I would have to read it since Miles Pollack has died. I remember telling myself to hide it well, but then I forgot what I did with it in the confusion of moving."

"You're going to have to think hard about this one. I will help with the cleanup tomorrow."

"I must see my mother first before she hears about this from some other source, either at Eden Court or from Debbie or Jerry. It's bound to be on the news."

"Why don't I take you there tomorrow?"

"I feel guilty about intruding so much on your time but okay."

"Why feel guilty? I like spending time with you, even if it's a little more exciting than I would have imagined."

Catharine forgot her dilemma in this moment of Aaron's affirmation. She felt secure with him as a friend and maybe more than a friend in the future.

❧

By the next day, the whole town knew about the break-in. If not through the grapevine, they heard about it on the local radio station.

When Catharine arrived at her office a few minutes before eight, work colleagues and students alike expressed their concern and asked questions she couldn't answer, such as, "Why?"

Miriam Koster called her at the office after the last class. "I'm going to help you clean up the cottage," she said. "When would you like me to be there?"

"Thank you. First, I want to visit my mother at Eden Court before this news gets to her. She would be horrified. I should be back by three, and you have a key."

"I've already ordered a new mattress to be delivered on Friday, so you may want to stay at Verona's for another night, or you're welcome to stay with me."

"Thank you, thank you, Miriam. You're so thoughtful. I wouldn't have even thought about ordering a mattress. I'll pay you for it later."

"No, no. This wasn't your fault."

I'm not so sure.

Aaron entered the office as she closed her cell phone. "Are you ready for our trip to Eden Court?"

"Yes, in a couple of minutes."

Catharine's few minutes turned into half an hour as she straightened her desk and took essays to be read.

When they arrived at Eden Court, Emma, the receptionist, had already heard the news on the local radio station, and Catharine affirmed it.

"How is Mama? She didn't hear about it, did she?"

"No," said Emma.

"She does seem happier after your cousin came by yesterday though."

"Oh good. So Jerry and Debbie came to visit?"

"No, I mean the cousin visiting from Ohio. Too bad she

wasn't able to remember him, but he was friendly and helped her mood."

"Cousin from Ohio? What was his name?

"Let me look at the visitor's sheet. Um, looks like he didn't sign in. He said his name was Don something."

"I don't have any cousins in Ohio!" She rushed into her mother's room.

Her mother sat up in the bed, beaming. "Hello, Catharine. I'll be so glad to get out of here."

"Who was your visitor? A cousin? Had you ever seen him before?"

"Catharine, you know my memory isn't good, but he said he will get me out of here."

"What else did he say?"

"I told him about you and the family. He seemed interested in you and said you had family historical documents he wanted to get. He said to tell you to have them ready."

Catharine sat speechless.

Aaron entered the room and saw the ashen look on Catharine's face.

"Someone has been here," she said. "I'll be right back, Mama."

"We need to talk." Aaron followed her to the lobby.

In the solitude of the empty lobby, she said, "I think she has been threatened, but she doesn't know it. She needs a twenty-four-hour guard."

"What's going on?"

"Come with me." They walked to the other end of the lobby, to Emma's desk.

"Emma, tell Aaron what you told me about a cousin visiting Mama from Ohio."

Emma repeated the story, and Catharine added information

she'd gotten from her mother. They returned to her mother's room and had her repeat her version for all of them.

"Mama, we don't have any cousins in Ohio. If this man comes back again or calls you, do not talk to him. We will let Emma know not to let him in."

Her mother shook her head, looking confused. "Who was he?"

"I don't know, Mama, but we're going to find out."

Out in the lobby, Aaron called Zeph.

"I'll be right there," Zeph said.

Thirty minutes later Zeph walked in briskly with an air of importance. Emma described the visitor as a distinguished-looking older man, probably in his sixties, with a trimmed grayish beard. He wore a brown business suit, a light-blue shirt, and a beige tie.

"I couldn't help noticing how well he was dressed," she said.

Aaron turned to Catharine. "Do you have a picture of Dr. Kushner?"

"No, I don't."

"Tell me what you know about him. Have you met him? What does he look like?"

"My only meeting with Raymond Kushner was at a physics conference in San Diego about five years ago. I remember this slightly overweight, balding, older man wandering up and down the exhibit hall. I noticed that his suit seemed too large for him, as if he might have lost some weight and hadn't bought a better-fitting one. Kenji pointed him out as Dr. Kushner, the director of the institute.

"Later he came up to shake hands with Kenji and complimented him on his 'beautiful wife.' He took my hand and held on to it in a sexist manner, as some old men do. He had a New York accent and seemed friendly enough. Then he said I looked like a career woman and asked what I did. When I told him I was a theology professor, he just sort of grunted and turned away. He's more than sixty years old now. I'm sure he is well into his seventies. If it wasn't him, I'll bet he had something to do with this incident."

Chapter 21

Catharine couldn't help herself. She knew it wasn't the appropriate thing to do under the circumstances, but when they arrived at the cottage after class, she took her cell phone into the bathroom and dialed the Physics Institute.

"Is Dr. Kushner in?"

"No," said the receptionist, "he retired last fall."

"I see. Is he still in the area?"

"I don't know. Who is this?"

"It doesn't matter. Thank you." Catharine closed the cell phone with a snap.

She remembered what Kenji had said. *If something should happen to me, put this in a safe place and don't let anyone have it. It has to do with politics at the institute. After two years, give it to the name on the envelope. By then some things will have changed.*

Did he mean Kushner would be gone? And if he was gone, would it mean he was acting alone to find the research?

Catharine waited a few minutes, analyzing the new information, then went to help get the cottage in shape.

By seven o'clock in the evening, the cottage looked neat, vacuumed, and dusted, with all its furniture upright. She thanked Miriam; James, a work colleague who had come to help; and Aaron. They had put the foodstuffs back on the pantry shelves and cleaned up glass from the kitchen and pantry floors. The culprits had searched everything, including the clothes hanging in her closet, some of which had fallen to the floor. Catharine was thankful none of Miriam's antique furniture had been damaged.

"Let's go for some pizza on me," said James, and they piled into his SUV for a trip into town. These were her friends, so Catharine shared some of her information with them, being careful not to involve Ralph Brown. She told them she thought the intruders had been looking for research work her husband had done at the institute. Aaron later said she had shared too much, but Catharine prided herself in being transparent.

She felt more at ease now.

Zeph called. "I wanted to let you know one of my men will stake out Eden Court. I've alerted the administration and support staff of the situation. The police will also put the cottage on their regular lookout route around the county. You'll be glad to hear that I cannot arrest Ralph Brown unless you ask us to charge him with writing the threatening letter." She wouldn't.

Catharine drove her own car to Verona's and enjoyed a warm bath in their Jacuzzi. After meditation and prayer, she fell asleep. Tomorrow was Friday, then the weekend.

The following morning's rush included having breakfast early with the Jenkinses, checking out, and taking Chiro to the cottage. The cat stepped out of his cage cautiously, looking around. She gave him some treats and sped out the door.

Catharine arrived at work late again, just before the beginning of the Hebrew class. Aaron had left a message earlier, saying he wouldn't be seeing her until Sunday, because he needed to catch up on his class work. She understood; she had essays in her briefcase to be read, so she had to apologize to her second class.

"It's been a busy week, as you know," she told them. "I will have the essays ready by Monday."

After class and without lunch, she left for Eden Court, skipping the gym again. Her mother seemed a bit disoriented, and Catharine didn't stay long, saying she would be back Sabbath afternoon to read the Bible to her. It wasn't that her mother couldn't see to read—she had large-print material; she just liked to hear Catharine read.

In the evening she called Aaron to discuss solving the mystery, but he told her it might not be safe to talk about it on the phone. "I could stop over."

"No," said Catharine. "Let's keep it till Sunday. I'll have lunch ready here at noon."

"Meanwhile think about where that letter might be."

∽

Catharine rose earlier than usual Sunday morning. She admitted to herself that she had missed Aaron on Friday and Saturday. She chastised herself for getting so obsessed with him. *I might get hurt. I fear disappointment. Disappointment is like seeing a flash of color in a field and running up, thinking of flowers; then when you get there, it is only trash someone has pitched. No, this would be worse than disappointment.*

She prepared a walnut-lentil roast; shitake mushroom gravy; greens sautéed with olive oil, peppers, garlic, and onions; baked potatoes; and pumpkin pudding. A really healthy meal, she told him. Aaron searched the cottage for a bug the burglars might have planted. Catharine laughed, finding the idea absurd.

"If connected with the institute, these are highly intelligent men," he said.

"And women," she added.

They spent the afternoon discussing the events of last week and new clues.

"That letter might tell us what they are looking for and where it is," Catharine concluded.

"You know what?" Aaron spoke in a whisper. "Maybe Kenji went to Edmonton to hide his papers with Mae, because they wouldn't have known about her."

"Yes, it could be."

"But I wish we could afford a private investigator to check on Kushner as well."

"Maybe we should go to the farmhouse this afternoon and check around there."

"Okay, get your coat."

When they parked outside the house, Catharine couldn't find her key. During the week she had changed her purse to a large, deep bag to hold the papers for her Bible study to keep them separate from her class work. She had taken it to the church on Wednesday night.

"It's probably at the bottom of the bag. I'm going to need to dump it out on the seat."

Aaron got out of the car and stood outside as a cascade of papers, pens, change purses, a wallet, and smaller items fell on the seat. Still things stuck inside. She pulled an envelope from the bottom of the bag.

It was the envelope with Miles Pollack's name on it.

CHAPTER 22

Catharine and Aaron looked at each other in disbelief, then stared at the envelope.

"Are you ready to open it?" he said.

"Here?"

"It's as good a place as any. First, let me dump this mess back into the black hole it came out of so I can sit in the car."

Catharine realized the letter had been in this bag since she used it on the move to Pennsylvania. When she'd changed to a smaller purse later, the letter had stayed in the bottom of the bag in her closet. But on Wednesday evening, when she changed to a bag to hold her copious notes, the letter had gone with her to church. The other purses in the closet had been opened and searched.

"Aaron, you open the letter and read it to me." She heard her voice tremble.

With a pocketknife, he slit the envelope and took out a sheet of paper. He gazed at the heading and began to read.

Dear Miles:

I am writing this letter should anything happen to me. Sometimes I fear for my life. As I told you,

Kushner and his cronies will do everything they can to keep my research from seeing the light of day, let alone published (should I even be able to find a journal open enough to consider it). It would bring the scientific world's current dating methods into question and shake up their concept of macroevolution. It could be like manna from heaven for believers. Only you and I know where this material is located.

I am giving this letter to Catharine to keep for me. So I don't put her in possible danger, I am asking her not to open it but to give it to you in two years should I not be around. By then Kushner will be retired, and a new, less volatile, cool-headed administration should be in charge at the institute. Otherwise I am biding my time until it is safe to present. Although Kushner wants desperately to get his hands on my papers and research records, I do not think he will do anything to get them while he is still director of the institute. He won't want to embroil them in controversy.

After he leaves, I am going to need your legal expertise in presenting and protecting my work. The opposition will not all be gone with Kushner, but there will be enough honest people to stand by me. At the same time, I will probably lose my job and more. No matter what, I am willing to face all the tribulation ahead. I can only pray Catharine will be up to it as well. Most of all, I want her protected.

Obviously our visit in Canada didn't quite go as I had expected. My personal life has taken a hit, yet it will all work for good. I believe Catharine will be strong enough to take the news. I will need your help with these new issues. But I will be talking to you about it long before you get this letter.

Sincerely,

"Well, what do you think, Catharine?"

"I guess he's talking about the visit to Edmonton and where he hid the papers."

"I'm betting on it."

&

On the way home, Catharine found herself seeing the whole story as pertaining to another woman in a mystery novel. She felt she had left her past, and the present belonged to someone else, to someone she didn't know.

"I know this is a private matter, but would you mind me asking some questions about your relationship with Kenji?" asked Aaron.

"Like what?"

"This was a cross-cultural marriage, and I'm wondering how much of your relationship may have differed from a traditional Western one. Was he domineering or controlling?"

"Kenji may have been the stereotypical dominant Japanese male when I think back on it. But I wouldn't have known, because I had no other man to compare him with besides my father. I had never even been kissed by any other male. Sometimes I wondered about Kenji's insistence on being the decision maker in purchasing furniture, cars, and home items. But my father also made those choices because he worried about money. And Kenji liked to be waited on, and my mother waited on my father. Kenji took care of finances but never denied me money. We had only one checking account, but he was generous with it, and we both gave a lot away."

"He treated you well?"

"Yes, we rarely argued. But he often treated me like a child, because of my ADD, by reminding me of things. He strictly disciplined Matt, and we sometimes argued about it. Though highly intelligent, Matt needed motivation as a teen.

"Kenji supported my career choice and education. He thought I was intellectually smart. His two sisters are educated. One is a pediatrician, and the other is a teacher. He planned ahead for Matt's education and encouraged his choice of medicine as a career."

"Do you think he kept things from you?"

"I wasn't aware of it, but evidently he did. He didn't talk about his work but physics and science in general. We discussed theology a lot. I enjoyed his interest in my field."

She looked away and came back to Aaron's original question. "I really don't know if secrecy is a trait of Japanese culture or not."

The news of Kenji's first marriage had made her feel devastated and betrayed, but the anger began to melt away. Talking about it helped. She could understand why he hadn't told her. Even so, one sentence in the letter left an empty feeling inside as she contemplated what it could mean and whether it mattered anymore. *I believe Catharine will be strong enough to take the news.*

CHAPTER 23

March continued to hold on to winter, with a few warm days scattered across its calendar. It finally left with warm lamblike temperatures melting all the snow, even in the darkest niches of the county. Crocuses bloomed, and daffodils unfolded their bright yellow faces along the roadways and on the Koster estate. The Lenten flowers by the cottage came to life, and their large, dark-green leaves, flattened by cold temperatures, were replaced with shoots pointing heavenward. Small, green leaves sprouted on trees everywhere.

Passover and Easter came and went. Catharine and Aaron celebrated Easter at church with music and a resurrection sermon. Catharine coordinated a Passover meal with her Hebrew and Bible students.

March passed without any threatening events. Catharine's mother didn't beg to go home as much, but she entered a happier phase. Whether it was because of increasing periods of memory loss or decreasing homesickness, Catharine didn't know. Her mother happily greeted Catharine, Debbie, Jerry, and their sons. She welcomed the little boys with her old love and enthusiasm. Her neighbor, Josie, and her church members visited frequently and brought flowers and other gifts.

Mama liked Aaron from the first time she met him. She once asked Catharine whether they would get married. "No, Mama," she said. "We've never even discussed it."

Occasionally Mama asked about her daughter, Sarah; and Catharine told her Sarah had called to ask about her. In reality there had been only two calls since Mama had been at Eden Court.

Although Catharine had talked to her sister in Florida at the time their mother fell, Sarah's follow-up had seemed sparse. This silence exacerbated a long-held resentment. *Doesn't she even care a little? Why is she so distant? She hasn't been here in years.*

Catharine's sister's lack of interest in family had angered her in the past, but this seemed unforgivable. Negative thoughts whirled around in her brain as she finished exercising one Friday in April. They continued as she walked home to prepare for Sabbath.

During her Saturday visit, Catharine decided to confront her mother about Sarah. "Why has Sarah been so distant from the family all these years, Mama?"

Her mother's frown accentuated the furrows between her eyes. "I think it has to do with Rachel," she said.

"Rachel, the baby who died in infancy?"

"Yes, Sarah looked forward to her birth as much as I did. She was born at home and probably didn't get as much care as she should have. I don't know. They call it SIDS these days when a baby dies suddenly like Rachel did."

"You mean Sarah took it hard?"

"Sarah had sung to her in her crib and kissed her good night. Rachel died some time before morning. Sarah's personality changed. She became sad, then scared, then seemed to forget, but something was different. Maybe it was because she was becoming a teenager, but she stopped talking to us. Your father and I didn't speak of Rachel again. Maybe that was wrong.

"When you came along, she acted like she couldn't have cared less. Then as a teenager, she got hard to handle. She refused to move with us to Pennsylvania. She married Doug, got divorced in a year, and went to work in a department store while attending art school. Sarah felt resentful we couldn't help much with money. We didn't have it.

"Then she met Vince at an art exhibit. He fell in love with her; they got married. He was rich, and he helped her finish art school. They visited us once a year when George was little, now not at all."

"Are they happy, Mama?"

"Who knows?"

♪♪

In the evening Aaron came by, and Catharine told him about her poor relationship with Sarah. "Teasing seemed to be the only way she related to me. I remember one time when we were at home alone. Sarah liked to set up this large blackboard and create pictures with colored chalk, a treat when the family was together. But if Mama and Daddy were out when Sarah set up her blackboard, I got frightened. One day in the dining room while we played dominoes, Sarah said she was bored and went to get her blackboard.

"'Now, let's see what we can bring to life today' she said with this wicked smile. In no time, Sarah drew the scariest monster.

"I still remember her saying, 'See, he has blood dripping from his long fingernails,' and he did—I can see it still today. I screamed and ran out of the room. Sarah chased me, laughing and holding the drawing in front of her. Then we heard our parents open the front door. I saw Sarah sweep her arm across the picture, transferring the monster to the sleeve of her shirt. She destroyed the evidence, but I felt like the monster was still there on her shirt."

123

"She sounded immature for an eighteen-year-old. Did she ever live at the farm?"

"No, the next spring, before my fourth birthday, we moved to Pennsylvania to live at Jacob's Farm after Grandfather Jacob Weaver died. Sarah refused to come with us. Against our parents' wishes, she married a man she knew for only two weeks. She stayed in Baltimore, went to work, and quit her art classes. But the marriage didn't last; he was abusive. She went out on her own, rented a room, worked in a department store, and took art lessons at night after work. Later she met Vince at an art exhibit, and I guess it was love at first sight. She was beautiful."

"She must have been a talented artist, too," said Aaron.

"Yes, even before art school, she painted our screens in Baltimore."

"Screens?"

"Yes, we lived in a row house identical to the others on our street. Painted screens kept them from looking ordinary. A Baltimore tradition, homeowners hired local artists to create colorful scenes on the screen doors or windows. They became art pieces for windows opening onto the sidewalk and blocked the view into the front room while residents could see out. I read that a few still exist in some parts of the city but only a couple of artisans.

"Sarah painted a tropical vista of flowers and palm trees for our screen door. Even at the age of three, I used to sit in front of it and imagine myself in the scene. She did the window screens too, painting a bowl of red roses on the middle one and some vines on the other two."

"Wow, do you have any of her work?"

"All I have is a colorful sketch of a windmill she did before I was born." Tears welled up in Catharine's eyes and rolled down her cheeks.

"You do love her, don't you?"

"Of course, I remember how she taught me games like checkers, marbles, and dominoes. We had fun. I miss her in my life."

Chapter 24

Three days with rain seem worse than thirty days without it, thought Catharine. The heavy drops resounded on the metal roof of the cottage with a steady beat all day.

On the third day of April showers, Catharine sat at her desk, preparing for her next class when the phone rang. The name coming up on the screen surprised her: "Julian Mills." Why would he be calling? Dr. Mills was the director of the Biblical Languages Department, where she had previously taught. He had been her supporter and friend for years. His wife had divorced him three years ago, and he'd seemed lonely during the last year she was at the seminary.

"Hello, Catharine, this is Julian. I've been wondering how you were doing."

"Hello, Julian," she said and gave him a brief summary of her work at the college. "And how about you?"

"Well, I'm good, but we miss you here." He went on to talk about some changes since she had left.

"Why I'm really calling," he said, "is that I hear there is great fishing up there. Fishing is my hobby, and I wondered, if I came up, could you show me some fishing spots? I'm taking off a couple of days for some R & R."

"It depends on what days you have in mind. I teach every weekday, and on Saturday, as you remember, I go to church. What about a Sunday?"

"Yes, next Sunday would be perfect if the weather is good. It's raining here today."

"And here too. We're having heavy rain and some flooding of the creeks. Maybe the next Sunday would be better. I'll ask a friend about the best places for fishing and have him come along as a guide."

"You don't have to. I know all about fishing. You don't already have a boyfriend there, do you?"

"I have a friend—many friends actually," Catharine said. "One of them is a professor of biology; he knows where all the fishing holes are."

"Umm, okay," he said. "I do want to talk to you alone at some point. I'll take you out to dinner." Without waiting for an answer, Julian went on to make plans for a week and a half later and said good-bye.

At lunch the next day she told Aaron about the proposed fishing trip. He seemed a little quiet and finally asked whether this was someone she had dated.

"Oh, no," she said. "As the department head, I would never have done so, even if he had asked, which he didn't. I have no such interest in him. I find him a bit too controlling actually."

"I hope he doesn't tell me how to fish."

"He probably will."

❧

The Sunday of the fishing trip dawned, sunny and balmy with a clear sky, an unusual occurrence for the valley. Aaron planned a trip to at least two fishing places; there were many to choose from in the county. He also suggested giving Julian a tour of the area.

Catharine hated early mornings, being a genetic night owl. But she pulled herself out of bed at five o'clock in the morning to indulge in a rare cup of coffee and have some ready for the two men.

Julian arrived, dressed as if he'd stepped out of *Field & Stream.* According to him, fishing has to begin early in the morning, so he knocked on the cottage door at six, the exact moment he said he would. Aaron came five minutes later, wearing the typical hip boots, old jeans, and a flannel shirt.

They had eaten breakfast and carried thermoses of coffee. Catharine chastised herself for not inviting them for breakfast. They wasted no time in getting out the door.

The first spot was one of Catharine's favorite places, the Singing Bridge over Tuscarora Creek near Academia. "The Singing Bridge got its name from the sound elicited from the metal ties when a vehicle drove over it," she told Julian.

They made a couple of unsuccessful casts off the Singing Bridge and moved on to a bridge farther up the creek. This concrete bridge gave them a good view of one of Juniata County's tourist attractions, a long wooden-covered bridge running parallel and upstream from the roadway's bridge. "It's known as the Academia Bridge, and it dates back to 1902. It's a two-span bridge with vertical siding and open windows at the eave level, and at two hundred seventy feet, it's one of the longest of the remaining covered bridges in Pennsylvania," Aaron told them.

Julian took several photos of it. "I want to do an oil painting of the covered bridge," he informed them.

Julian prepared his rod and took from an impressive bag all sorts of lures, hooks, and other gear; he waded into the river along with Aaron. Catharine stayed on the bridge, watched the two men, and walked up and down the empty road for what seemed like hours. Near one end of the bridge sat a tiny vine-covered cottage.

She remembered a young couple who had once lived there back in the late sixties. They'd sold jarred honey to the local people from their own bees. They'd come here as part of a small Hare Krishna settlement, probably long gone. But her thoughts were interrupted when she turned a corner and saw a "Yoga Camp" with buildings and symbols all indicative that the sect had never left the area. She told Julian about them later when they passed the camp.

"They have all kinds here, huh?" he said.

"I attended their vegan lunches several times," Catharine said.

"You've got to be kidding!" he said, shaking his head.

The fishing results were minimal, with only a couple of small bass the men threw back. So they drove to the Juniata River. On the way, Julian bragged about the large fish he'd caught in California last fall in the stocked lakes around Lake Arrowhead. "We used cheese on treble hooks, and I caught several twenty-inch trout."

Their luck improved in the Juniata River. While Julian used his colorful lures, Aaron used worms that seemed more appetizing to the fish. He placed his fish in a bucket of water to keep them fresh, while Julian put his in an expensive-looking creel. The day was heading toward lunchtime, and they were about to quit when Julian hooked a beautiful nineteen-inch smallmouth bass using a yellow lure on his ultralight line.

He was excited about his catch and had Catharine take several pictures of it.

"Our local paper publishes photos each week of a fisherman and his or her catch. Maybe I could submit this for you," she said.

Julian jumped at the idea. "Submit it for me, will you? And send me the whole paper."

She laughed. "Of course I will."

Julian offered to take them out to lunch. Catharine guessed he hoped Aaron would bow out and go home, but he didn't.

"Sure, I'll come along and take you on a short tour of the area," Aaron said.

After the men removed their boots and packed their fishing gear, they went to a local restaurant. She felt uncomfortable as Julian talked about his career accomplishments, and Aaron stayed quieter than usual.

When they got back into the car, Julian asked Aaron to drive. "You know the place, and I would really like to sit with Catharine and talk about old times, if you don't mind. I mean, while we are on the way to these places," he said. "I haven't seen her for a while."

Catharine looked at Aaron, who pursed his lips and said, "Sure."

"Drive up to her farmhouse first. I've heard so much about it. Let's start north," he directed, "and come down to the southern part of the county and go back to the college."

During the drive, Julian talked to her in a low voice, leaving Aaron out of any conversation. He talked of people they knew back in Washington and places to visit, emphasizing what a great cultural place it was to live in, as though she hadn't spent more than ten years there.

She noticed Julian was indeed handsome with a gorgeous shock of white hair. She thought he must be about sixty with all his experience, but he didn't look it. He kept in shape and didn't have the male-trunk obesity typical of his age. However, she felt no attraction to him and found him rather pompous.

"You know, we could find a place for you again next school year. I would think by this time that you've gotten a bit bored here—it's not you, Catharine. With your mother now in a nursing home, you could leave. And I personally miss you." He took her hand, gave it a squeeze, and didn't let go. She wondered whether she should jerk her hand away and insult him or leave it there. While he continued talking, she gradually pulled her hand away.

After looking at the farm—they didn't go into the empty house—Aaron turned the car around, and they left. "It's country all right," Julian said.

Next they drove up to the Mennonite Historical Center, a square brick building with a weathered spire sitting atop a steep hill and surrounded by gravestones on two sides. "It used to be a church, the one where my great-great-grandparents attended and are buried. All of my ancestors' lives are recorded here since they came from Switzerland. Ancestry is quite important to Mennonites." When Catharine started to tell him about her family, he interrupted to tell her about how his family had come from English royalty.

"If you like genealogy, you would enjoy seeing the magnificent estates where they once lived in England," he said.

Catharine wondered why he thought she should be interested in his ancestors.

Aaron pointed out the old courthouse in Mifflintown and other historical places. They took a side trip to the site of the Women's Academy and museum on the way back to the college. "It burned down mysteriously in the 1800s, and some claim the ruins are haunted by those who perished in the fire," he said. They returned to the campus and rode around as Aaron pointed out various buildings.

When they arrived at her cottage, Catharine presumed Julian would be on his way and didn't invite him in. He did, however, invite himself.

"Can I come in for a few minutes?" he said.

"Of course, if you have time. Aaron, I have your favorite chocolate chip cookies made." She held her hand out to him, and he took it.

Julian noticed the gesture and added, "I would like to get back before dark."

The two men talked while Catharine fixed some herb tea and more coffee. She brought out a large plate of her homemade chocolate-chip oatmeal cookies and set it before them. She and Aaron ate most of them. Julian had only one.

Julian didn't say any more about returning to Washington until he was ready to leave. "Remember, Catharine, you can come back anytime. By the way, I'm sorry to hear about Kenji's lab assistant. I recognized his name in the paper right away, Marti Gaston. I recall meeting him once when I came to your house for dinner."

"What are you talking about?" she said as her eyes widened.

"You may not have heard he was in a fatal accident last week. He went off the road and hit a tree. His injuries weren't bad, but the paper said he had a heart attack while driving."

"A heart attack? He was only thirty-two years old!"

"I know. I'm sorry to give you such bad news." He looked at her with sympathy in his eyes. "I must go, my dear Catharine." He leaned over and kissed her on the cheek. "Glad to have met you, Aaron." He shook Aaron's hand and nodded to Catharine. "She's a special lady. Take care of her."

♪♪

Catharine didn't miss the significance of what Julian had said, but she was distracted and angry over Marti. "He couldn't have had a heart attack. He used to run with Kenji," she screamed, then sobbed relentlessly. "They killed them; I know they killed them. I can't stand this anymore. I've had enough. They'll kill us."

Aaron ran to her and hugged her so tightly she gasped for breath. "You're okay, we're okay," he said soothingly. He led her to the couch, and over the next ten minutes he held her as she conquered the panic and got control of her emotions.

"I'm sorry I lost it," she said.

"You've been through a lot lately; you have a right to be hysterical," he said and smiled. He reached over and kissed her on the lips. The delicious feel of his lips not only stopped her angst but also gave her feelings she hadn't experienced in years.

She hugged him, and he rubbed his cheek against hers, his eyes closed.

"Kiss me again, Aaron."

He stood up suddenly. "No, Catharine, you're too vulnerable right now. I'd better go; you're okay. Should you have another panic spell, just breathe into a paper bag, and it will subside." He squeezed her hand as he left. "You can also call me."

જાર

The following day at Catharine's campus office, a package came from the mail room, requiring a signature. Puzzled, she signed for it, then had to sit down. The package was from Marti Gaston. Its postmark was dated one week earlier.

Catharine gingerly opened the package. Inside she found Kenji's missing journals. A hastily written note was under a rubber band on the first one. It said,

> Catharine: I found these at the institute. I know they belong to you. I'll give you a call soon. I am leaving the institute. Marti.

CHAPTER 25

Catharine took the journals to the cottage and hid them in her closet. *Not that they will be safe there*, she told herself. She called Aaron and told him about the package.

"You're right, Cat. The institute is involved big-time in your life. Maybe they did tell Ralph to go after you."

"I have always believed it," she said. "I did some computer sleuthing and found poor Marti had his accident the day after he mailed the package."

"How are you holding up?"

"I'm fine. Really. No more fearfulness. My trust is in my Lord. He has given you as my friend and support. My mother is well for ninety-three. My son and family are great. I am blessed."

"On another subject, remember the photo of Julian holding his nineteen-inch trout? Well, the picture came out, but next to him is the photo of a local boy with a thirty-inch musky. Should I still send the whole paper to him or just the photo?"

Aaron laughed mercilessly. "Poor guy. I would send the paper, but you're so softhearted. You'll send only the photo, right?"

"Right."

"Now, I called because I'm under some pressure. I keep hearing rumors about my class; some think I am teaching evolution, and they say it disturbs the parents and confuses the students."

"I'm sorry. Let's talk about it soon, probably not in the cafeteria though."

ↄ♫ↄ

On Wednesday afternoon, as Catharine was working at home, the phone rang. The noise startled Chiro from his spot next to the phone, and he complained in a clipped "meow-ik."

Catharine grabbed the phone. "Hello?"

"Hi, Cat. Can I stop over this afternoon? I need to talk to you." It was Aaron.

"Sure," she replied, wondering about the urgency in his voice.

Not more than fifteen minutes later, Aaron came to the door, and Catharine opened it as he pushed his way in, looking rather unhappy.

"I need to talk to someone," he said. "I may be losing my job." He took off his suit jacket, folded it, and placed it on a chair. "Remember what we talked about Monday?" he said as he paced the floor.

"Yes, your problem about teaching evolution." She had avoided the subject, since she remembered creation science debates with him in the past. He'd argued for the Darwinian theory without sharing his personal opinion.

"What happened? Is something wrong?"

"I'm afraid so. Dr. Ruben Kline, the physician in Mifflin, complained to the administration about the Biology Department and my role in it. He says we're teaching evolution to our students, and we should all be replaced with believing Christians. He wants a meeting with the board of trustees."

"Are you, Aaron? Teaching evolution, I mean?"

"Of course. I prepare students for the real world. How are they going to react when faced with the concept and discover they don't know enough about it to sound intelligent? Some of these kids plan to go to graduate school in the sciences!"

"Yes, I understand. But there are two kinds of evolution—macro and micro—and we need to acknowledge micro, but macroevolution undermines our faith as Christians."

"I don't believe it needs to," Aaron huffed. "There are many Christians who are scientists and accept a gradual evolution directed by God."

Catharine was uncomfortable asking whether he was one of them.

"Just what has Dr. Kline claimed? He is, after all, just one person. Are there others?"

"I'm afraid so. He's got a following, and some are parents. I'm told this could keep religious families from sending their kids here. Some people in this part of the country don't think a college education is worth having anyway, and academia is Babylon."

"How did you hear about this? Were you particularly mentioned by Dr. Kline?"

"Yes, he did mention me by name. I have had his daughter in my class this year. When we come here to teach, we sign a statement of belief, asking whether we accept Christ as our personal Savior, and of course I do. But now I'm accused of undermining the Christianity of my students by teaching evolution, and supposedly I have been doing this for five years!"

"What does the administration say?"

"Dr. Bonheller told me we will need to meet and draw up a statement. He is supportive of us, but Kenny isn't, and Kenny is his boss." Aaron continued with anxiety in his voice, "Kenny says if I'm being paid by the college, I must believe and teach as they do, and they believe in a real six-day creation, Noah's ark, and all the rest as literal."

Again Catharine wanted to ask whether he didn't.

Instead she said, "There's some truth to the idea that you shouldn't take money from an institution that promotes one way of thinking while you teach another. Is it ethical to accept their dollars while at the same time not sharing the majority belief?"

Aaron's eyes widened. "What?"

"I mean." She stopped and paused to think of what to say without making her sound like one of his enemies. "I mean, the underlying questions are simple."

"Oh, come on. None of this is simple. You're smart enough to know that!"

She looked him straight in the eyes and in rapid fire shot a volley of questions at him. "Do you or any of the instructors teach Darwinian evolution as gospel truth? Do you use it as a test in grading? Do you press the beliefs of macroevolution on the students and present a six-day creation as impossible? Do you make fun of those who believe it?"

He slammed his hand down on the desk and shouted, "No, no, no, no, and no!"

"Then what's the problem? Don't they want you to even tell what evolution is about?"

"It's not just that," he said, his eyes flaring. "They want to take away my academic freedom to believe according to my own conscience. They want me to say I accept every word of the Bible as literal truth. They call it inerrancy, but it's way beyond inerrancy."

"I see," she said. "Why don't you have a seat, and I'll get us some chamomile tea."

She crossed the open room to the kitchen area as Aaron sat on the couch. Chiro joined him and jumped up beside him as if to calm him. He scratched behind Chiro's ears and petted his ample form. Catharine brought two dainty, white gold-rimmed cups with tea bags and several homemade chocolate chip cookies. She set them on the coffee table.

They sat silently while Aaron sipped his tea.

"The problem, Aaron, is that Christianity can't be compatible with Darwinian evolution, which requires death and sin to exist before the fall in Eden. The Bible says God created the earth and Adam and Eve whole and perfect. Then they sinned and required a Savior because the 'wages of sin is death.'"

Aaron scowled. "Cat, I know you mean well in explaining all this to me, but right now I don't need Bible lessons." His voice grew more strident. "I'm just fed up with the accusations. This isn't the first time I've heard them, and now you're echoing some of the same stuff. Sometimes I don't know what I believe, but I'm teaching those kids that God exists and is part of their lives. I don't know what more they want of me. A Bible class?"

"Aaron, don't be so angry. It disturbs me."

"You don't understand, do you? I think I should go." He set the cup down and grabbed his jacket. "Thank you for the tea." His words were cool. He started for the door, stopped, turned, picked up a napkin, and scooped a mound of cookies into it. He left without a word.

Tears welled in Catharine's eyes. Turning to Chiro, she whispered, "I've said the wrong thing again."

She got up, walked to the kitchen, and polished off the rest of the chocolate chip cookies.

CHAPTER 26

An hour after he left, Aaron called and apologized for his behavior.

"I wanted you to listen, not question me," he said. "I'm already being questioned. I don't know if I said the right thing to Kenny when he called me into his office. I felt like a naughty child being called to the principal's office. It hurt because I had always considered George a good friend. We used to play racquetball together until he hurt his knee."

She could feel the frustration in his voice and responded to it. "I need to apologize too. I should have understood that when someone comes to you with a problem, they are asking to be listened to, not preached at."

"You got it right," he said.

She overlooked his chastisement. "I suppose you told him the importance of teaching Darwin's theory of life, because the students need it for graduate school?"

"Yes, I told him. There will be a special board meeting to discuss the charges and have the doctor and his daughter face us with their complaint. Norris, the geology teacher, is also being called in. It's set for Thursday, April twentieth. Meanwhile they'll interview other students in our classes to see if they thought we taught evolution as fact and if we ever suppressed or discounted belief in creationism."

"Did she say you did—I mean, discount creationism?"

"Yes, she made that charge, but I would never do so."

"This will need some prayer and soul-searching," said Catharine. "If you have doubts about what you teach, they will need to come out."

"I hear you. But how can they demand I not have questions about how creation came about in deep time?"

"I can't imagine an educational institution demanding one hundred percent acquiescence to literalism as they understand it. We will have questions until the second coming."

"Tell that to Kenny!"

"Can I take you to church tomorrow? Maybe your pastor has some ideas."

"Sorry, I don't think he'll be taking your side, Aaron."

"I suppose not."

"Yes, we are big on creationism and the six literal days. The seventh-day Sabbath is a memorial to creation because God rested from His work on that day. And Sabbath is a symbol of our rest in Jesus. I have heard it said that if humans had celebrated the original Sabbath all along, evolution wouldn't have been accepted so easily."

"Tell that to the Jews. Most of them are agnostic now."

❧

Aaron told Catharine at one of their lunch breaks, "Last school year I received vague complaints from other sources about teaching too much evolutionary theory. So I recorded all of my lectures on a digital recording device. I didn't tell the students or anyone else. It will take time, but I will have to listen to them. I labeled them by subject, which helps."

Over the next several days, Aaron listened to his recorded lectures relating to evolution. He could find none claiming the theory as a viable alternative to creationism.

"This project is time consuming, and I resent it," he said to Catharine the next time they met for lunch. "The school year ends in six weeks, and I have a lot to do."

"What kind of grades does the doctor's daughter make in your class?"

"She is a C student in my class. She requires a science for her curriculum, and I'm sure my C is bringing down her GPA."

"That would make her unhappy with you. But enough to lie?"

"We'll see on April twentieth."

Catharine changed the subject. "I have an idea for my next Bible study at church. I'm going to talk about Genesis. I won't directly invite my students but inform them if they want to come. What do you think?"

"Sure, sounds good to me."

"Will you attend?"

Across the table Aaron was skillfully cutting into a lamb chop, but she thought his long fingers grew tense.

She backed off. "I mean, you don't need to. I'm not pressuring you."

"I'll see how my homework checking is going and let you know before next week," he said.

CHAPTER 27

When April 20 came, Catharine skipped the gym and went home to pray. In prayer she talked to a Friend, especially necessary in desperate times. She loved Aaron and hoped their lives would intertwine in the future. If he left Midland, the separation would make their relationship difficult to sustain. She wanted him to have a faith that went beyond science and theories. He believed in Christ and the gospel, and they often prayed together.

But what about the dichotomy that exists in such a faith? If the miracle of creation is suspect, what about the resurrection? In no stretch of the mind can the raising of a man from the dead be proved in a human laboratory.

The contradiction had no easy solution. She herself struggled with the inerrancy of the Bible, something the college claimed necessary for an evangelical Christian. *With scientific dating on the age of life, how can a conservative church maintain a six-day creation belief and stay relevant and credible? And does it really matter? Isn't belief in God as Creator the priority? What about faith in Bible history? Had Kenji found an answer in his research on time?*

How much did Christ know about science? Any more than His peers? This led her to wonder, *How could Christ, with human feelings, fears, and doubts, see beyond the grave? Was He tempted, like all humans, to give up dependence on the Father? His salvation work was why He came here, and He finished it at the cross. He took His Sabbath rest in the tomb and rose to life eternal for us all.*

One needed faith in a God, who created from love and chose a primitive people to be His witness. Catharine wondered how one could believe in a God who created through the violence of tooth, claw, and death over millions of years.

❧❧

At five o'clock in the afternoon, the phone rang, and Catharine tripped over Chiro to get to it. Up in a flash, she got it on the last ring. "Aaron?"

"Yes, it's okay, and I have a story for you. I'll be over in ten minutes. Do you have something for sandwiches?"

In fifteen minutes, Aaron rushed in unceremoniously, as if entering his own home. He began his tale.

"Well, Brenda and her father were there, and they brought a recording of one of my lectures, which they said proved I promoted evolution. It basically explained similarities in various kinds of birds and how this could show evolution. I remembered the lecture and couldn't wait until the end. But then they stopped the tape and looked at me. The board also looked at me. They thought they had proof.

"Then I said, 'But that isn't all. You have to play the whole session.' The Klines said they didn't have any more on the disk. We had heard the lecture.

"I said, 'No, you don't have it all. Last year I recorded my classes on an electronic device, and I remember this one.' I got out my Sony, picked the labeled disk, and played it to the end of the session. Just as I remembered, at the end I told the class to know these things, because they will come up at any university science class they attend. I gave them an assignment to research and disprove what they'd heard."

"How clever," affirmed Catharine. "How did they respond?"

"The men on the board shook their heads, had a discussion, and adjourned the meeting. Dr. Kenny told me afterward that I should do research this summer to bolster my faith in the Bible. I have a meeting with him next week, but I think the incident is resolved. I don't believe they will give Norris a hard time either, as Kline has ruined his credibility with the board."

"The lesson on Genesis is on my agenda for next week. Want to come?" said Catharine.

"Sure."

Catharine spent the next several days studying and researching Genesis and evolutionary theory. It wasn't the first time she had done so; she had folders full of material and personal writings on the subject she had hoped to include in a book she and Kenji would have worked on together. Most set forth a powerful and mysterious God whose works go beyond human knowledge and a vast, mysterious cosmos.

Chapter 28

At the church study Catharine explained the meaning of creation and the theological complications of macroevolution. The creation story also had glitches. "Did creation happen in six literal twenty-four-hour days as Genesis 1 indicates, but Genesis 2 does not? For many the creation story lacks credibility, because it can't fit into the evidence for macroevolution. Dating methods are a barrier. So is the appearance of light before the sun is created. But Christ is referred to as the light of the world; everywhere God goes there is light.

"My husband researched space-time theory, and once said, 'Perhaps we need to start over in the past.' Because Genesis 1:2 doesn't mention time, many conclude God made the earth and the heavens before creation week; others believe the whole universe was made in six days. The texts following verse 2 tell us God's powerful Word created life. John 1:5 infers that Christ is the Word and the Light and the Creator. His light dispelled darkness and brought life."

There's so much more to present, but how to do it before this conservative group without them wondering if I'm teaching heresy?

After the church study, Aaron said, "Well, you made a good case for the conservative concept of creation."

She felt his comment to be noncommittal and lacking in enthusiasm, and he surprised her by asking her to present it to his biology classes. She couldn't be sure whether he meant this as an affirmation or a way to convince his students and administration of his orthodoxy.

Two days later she gave the lecture to a combined class of science students.

"Before I move into creation versus evolution, keep in mind that I am not a scientist and can't debate the specifics of macroevolution. This is true for most people. They believe it because they trust the gods of science. For me macroevolution isn't a coherent process for the genesis of life. Life is a mystery beyond the material.

"As a follower of Christ—believed by classical Christianity to be the Son of God and Son of Man—I claim him as Savior and substitute because His glorified body rose from the grave some two thousand years ago, as described by witnesses and writers of sacred history. This cannot be proved by contemporary scientific method any more than can the theory of macro-evolution or biblical creation. Yet it is the major belief of Christianity; without it there is no viable Christian faith.

"I hold up the Bible as a life manual. It changes us. It tells us what constitutes sin and how sin makes individual and corporate life miserable. It is a document to accept as a whole with guiding principles evident in every story. While rejection of its principles ultimately leads to death, its theme leads to Christ the Judeo-Christian Messiah who offers eternal life to all who have ever lived or will live. It serves as a letter from God, dwelling on the spiritual and relational rather than material things irrelevant to our destiny."

She talked about trusting the Bible despite its thousands of translations over the centuries, the world view of our spiritual ancestors, the creation story compared to twenty-first-century science, and recent creation thoughts that don't include macroevolution. "Remember," she said, "God has an adversary in the conflict of good and evil. He's not popular, but he's real."

Catharine ended by saying, "We see immense space where the heavenly world resides and space and time intersect. Has God generated many universes and rules them from a control room He calls heaven? Do angels travel through black or white holes to watch out for us? Is this any more irregular than an unintentional cosmos evolved by a system we don't comprehend? But like quantum physics, truth is stranger than our speculations. We haven't scratched the surface, especially about the elusive properties of time. I think most scientists would agree."

After the lecture, a dozen students lined up to ask questions. Catharine noticed that Aaron stood back away from the group. *I guess he doesn't want to be involved in the discussion*, she thought.

CHAPTER 29

"Well, we got through another crisis," said Catharine. "And you won't lose your job."

"At least until next time," Aaron said.

"You will take the creation course, won't you?"

"If I don't, they'll label me as a rebel, and my job will still be in jeopardy. You want me to go, don't you? Hoping I'll be persuaded?"

"You really get to the core of things."

"I value openness in my relationships, and I can usually see behind pretenses and call them out."

"Do you think I pretend?" she said.

"I know you're an honest Christian—no charade there. But I don't always know where I stand with you. I wondered about Julian Mills. You dismissed him, yet you let him visit. But when we got home and you took my hand and invited me in, I knew you liked me better." He smiled and gave her a hug. "Little gestures make a difference. But there are things we have to talk about. You know that, don't you?"

"Go ahead and talk," she said. "We obviously don't see doctrine from the same perspective. But I sometimes have the same questions you do."

"And you won't share those questions with me? Sounds like pretense."

"Maybe, but I share them in prayer, where they belong."

"Are you afraid your religious belief system might topple if you express doubts out loud with someone else?"

"No, Aaron! You've got me all wrong. I questioned all the time in seminary. It was very acceptable there."

"But with me you often defend your faith or preach."

"You may be right. I never thought about it. I saw it as witnessing for my faith."

"Cat, I don't want to be in a relationship of witnessing," he said, frowning and with an edge to his voice.

Catharine's heart seemed to fall to her stomach; the words hurt, and she couldn't reply.

His voice rose as he said, "I've been through this before!"

"What do you mean?"

"Mary's religion broke us up. I married a Baptist and wound up with a charismatic."

"What's wrong with being a charismatic?"

"It was an independent cultish group. *Cultish* is my term. I'm sure they never thought of themselves that way. I blame myself for not going as a family to the Baptist church, but religion wasn't on my agenda. When the boys came along, she took them to her new church, and she harassed me to go and told me I was lost."

"You never went?"

"A couple of times, but it wasn't for me. Made me think of an Enya song: 'You go there you stay forever, I go there I lose my way.' I would have lost my way subjected to such a pushy and emotional religion. I'm a scientist!"

Catharine kept her eyes locked on his as he talked.

"She laid papers, magazines, and books around, hoping

I'd read them. She feared a 'rapture' when good people would disappear, and I'd be left. She even had the kids scared."

Catharine didn't say anything, but she remembered a time when some in her church had put fear into the kids about the "close of probation." It wasn't a rapture, but it was "secret." You never knew when it might occur, and your destiny was sealed.

He continued, "I said we never learned that at Midland. We fought a lot over her religion."

"Who left first?"

"One holiday Mary packed up to visit relatives in San Jose, California. She took the boys and never came back, except to nearly empty the house when I was at work."

"She didn't tell you she wasn't coming back?"

"Yeah, she called and said she wanted a divorce 'to be free to fulfill her life.' The crazy thing is, a few years later, she stopped going to church and joined a new age group to 'find herself.' By then she was remarried, and the boys had moved out."

"I'm sorry, Aaron. How horrible to tell someone they're lost. I hope I've never inferred you have to believe as I do."

"Not exactly, but I guess I've been on my guard."

Catharine said, "I've seen all kinds of Christians do the same thing to their spouses. I wouldn't be too harsh on her group. It's just sad she gave up on Christianity. But maybe she hasn't. I'll put her on my prayer list."

"I just want you to know I cannot join your church to win you. It would be pretense."

"I wouldn't want you to."

"Your church has some attractive beliefs, but they get lost in the priority given to past traditions. And there doesn't seem to have been any doctrinal growth since the founders hammered out their unique beliefs more than a hundred years ago."

She ignored his criticism. "Aaron, I know you are a born-again Christian, and you understand the gospel. Are you willing to share where you are now?"

"I came back to God two years after the divorce. He ultimately led me here, and I'm still growing. Christ is my Savior, and I talk to Him every day. I believe the gospel story of His death and resurrection and how it saves me. I believe the Ten Commandments came from God, and we need to honor them."

"Those are all positive and simple truths, and I believe them too."

"On the negative side—for you—I accept the scientific evidence for evolution, and I don't think the more exotic Bible stories happened exactly as reported. But there's historical evidence for most biblical names and events God's people experienced and passed down for generations. But their world view differed greatly from ours today."

"True," Catharine said. "But give me an example."

"There's evidence of a flood, but not worldwide; their local world was all they knew."

"I've heard it before," she said.

"Can you accept me in spite of these beliefs?"

Catharine squelched her desire to preach and said, "I believe God uses stories to tell His truths. I wouldn't say the Bible events didn't happen, but they weave a tapestry of history about how God relates to humans, and the Messiah is the central thread."

"I can agree with most of what you said. But you didn't answer my question."

"Of course, I respect your beliefs. If you denied God, it would be a very different response," she said.

"I'm glad to hear you say it. But don't be afraid to disagree with me—how boring! There's a difference between honest debate and persuasion by belittling the other person."

"Yes, I understand. When I was in college, I occasionally got negative comments about my religion. And the women's dean objected to my dating Kenji. But most students affirmed us."

"Hey, I remember our graduation. After he got his diploma, Kenji kissed you, and the kids applauded. They knew how some of the staff viewed your dating."

She laughed. "We both had last names near the end of the alphabet and stood next to each other, and you were at the end."

"Is that prophetic or what?" He laughed. "But I haven't finished our talk."

The scared feeling returned to Catharine.

"Can you go against the grain and get involved with a 'nonbeliever,' I think they call them. You see, I recently read the book I borrowed on church beliefs. What if you wanted to teach in one of their schools? Would I be a problem?"

"I don't think so, and I wouldn't seek a job with strings attached. I do love you, Aaron."

It was the first time the word had been spoken.

"And I'm asking these things because I love you," he said.

"I have a question for you, if you want to answer it. Was religion the only thing breaking up your marriage?"

"No, a rift developed, and she wanted things I couldn't afford."

"And that's it?"

He hung his head and said softly, "No." Aaron paused. "No, there was a guy at the church. He had more influence over her than I did."

"An affair?"

"I heard it inferred from a concerned member at her church, but I never asked her. I didn't want to know. It doesn't matter now."

"I'm sorry. Divorce results in grief, and I know all about grief," Catharine said.

"It sure does. And when you think it's over and has slithered away like a snake, it turns around, raises its head, and bites you in the face."

"An interesting metaphor. With me it seemed like a boa constrictor crushing me. But one day it relaxed its grip, I could breathe again, and it slinked away."

Aaron rose, stretched, and took her hand. "Let's take a walk and watch the sunset. Logan's outside," he said.

Chapter 30

May is a delightful month in rural Pennsylvania. Fresh green leaves burst from the limbs of poplar, maple, oak, sycamore, and lesser known deciduous trees. The countryside is a panorama of bright-emerald meadows and forested mountains.

Writing in her journal on a Friday afternoon, Catharine noticed the date: one year ago she had come for her interview with Dr. Kenny and accepted his invitation to teach at Midland. The months had sped by, and she would be fifty-three on Sunday. Catharine continued to write in her daily journal.

I am intrigued by time. Time is an old man creeping along when you are a child, but the older you get, the younger he gets, from walking to jogging to running. One day he will run out on all of us, and time will no longer be our enemy.

A call from Aaron interrupted her thoughts. "I want to go to church with you tomorrow," he said. "Shall I pick you up in the morning at the usual time? Or are you teaching Sabbath school this week?"

"Actually I'm not. We have a special guest from the general conference of the church. He will teach Sabbath school and give the sermon. It should be good."

"I'll pick you up at nine a.m."

It was a pleasant surprise; Aaron hadn't been to church with her since Easter when they went to two churches. But he often attended the Thursday Bible study.

He continued, "Let's go to the Hemlock Park for a picnic on Sunday. The weather is supposed be nice. I'll bring the lunch, and we'll celebrate your birthday."

A gorgeous Sabbath day awaited them along with a superb sermon. Aaron got a taste of what sermons could be like outside small towns with one pastor and three tiny congregations to manage. Most of the month, these churches depended on laypersons for sermons. As a professor of theology, Catharine was disappointed the pastor hadn't asked her to give one. "A couple of the farmers in the church are opposed to 'women preachers.' I don't agree with them, but I don't want to stir them up," he explained.

Church members prepared a potluck lunch in honor of the guest speaker.

On Sunday morning Aaron came to the cottage, and they drove in his truck to the hemlock forest where they had gone eight months ago. Logan accompanied them, but he stayed on his best behavior. Logan had become used to Catharine and no longer jumped on her when they met. She still kept him away from Chiro, who stayed home alone.

They parked the pickup and prepared for the hike. It was nine o'clock in the morning on a perfect day. As they trekked along, Aaron took her hand, as he often did these days. He even started singing the Beatles song "I Want to Hold Your Hand." "Sing along," he told her.

"I can't carry a tune. You know that by now."

"You have a good voice. Follow me, and you will."

They sang every Beatles song they could remember and some they couldn't; then came Elvis songs. The time passed quickly, and they circled back to the truck.

"I'm not hungry yet; it's only eleven," said Catharine.

"Let's have some water and rest," he said, spreading a red plaid blanket over the crunchy forest floor and setting the food chest nearby. She noticed it looked larger than the one he'd used last fall. From a tall, silver cooler, he poured out a dish of water for Logan, who noisily lapped it, then filled two paper cups for themselves.

Catharine lay back on the blanket and gazed up through the hemlock branches to the azure sky. Aaron lay down beside her, closer than they had sat when they were here in September. She thought it a symbol of how much closer they had become over the winter.

Leaning on his elbow, he turned and made eye contact, saying, "It's been almost eight months since we came here for our first date. Aside from our discussion this week, do you think much about where our relationship is going?"

"Yes," she said, and he bent closer.

He gently pulled her face to his, and for the first time, they shared a long, passionate kiss.

He moved away enough to say, "I love you," and they kissed again.

"We've spent a lot of time together since you came to Midland. Could you possibly imagine spending the rest of your life with me, Cat?" Aaron said.

"Of course, I'm in love with you, Aaron."

"I know," he said. "I have something to give you." He reached over for his jacket and removed an object from the pocket—a small black velvet box. At the sight of it, she knew what it contained, and her heart pounded.

"I've had this for a couple of weeks, waiting for your birthday." He opened it, displaying a sparkling diamond-and-gold ring.

Catharine flushed as she put out her left hand, and Aaron placed the ring on her ring finger.

She stared at it in shock. She was unprepared for the ring and at the same time overcome with feelings for him.

"Will you … ?" he said.

"Yes, yes, yes." She hugged him.

She wasn't sure how long they spent making out like teenagers, when Aaron reminded her that they needed to eat lunch. He pulled the large lunch container over and opened it up to reveal a special catered meal their favorite restaurant in Lewistown had prepared. Logan, who had been napping all this time, came alert with hungry eyes on the cardboard boxes inside.

"You really had all this planned, didn't you?"

"Of course."

CHAPTER 31

On the way home, they talked of wedding plans. "I would like to get it over with soon so we can travel and do some investigating, like a trip to Edmonton by train," Aaron said. "There's no necessity for a big wedding. We can go away and get married."

"I'll need to think about it," Catharine said. "I have a friend from the seminary in DC who is an ordained Methodist minister. Her name is Rev. Mary Katharine McKay. I would like her to perform the ceremony. Since Mama couldn't travel down there, she would come up here."

"I've got it! We can get married at Eden Court in the chapel. Your cousins and my buddy, James, could be our witnesses."

"There are so many people I would like to include, like our work colleagues and people from church and even my students." She laughed, saying, "In the college chapel and invite the whole campus!"

"Stop, stop," he said. "I know you're joking, right?"

"Of course. Why would we spend that kind of money for a few minutes?"

"Sounds like a huge ceremony for second timers."

"Yes, I wouldn't like making it a big thing either. We have until school is out in June to decide."

Catharine got out a calendar, and together they decided on a date in the middle of June.

"I'll call Mary Katharine and Laitha. I'll tell Sarah, even though she won't come, and our hiking friends and Matt and Carol in California. I think announcements would suffice for others."

"I'm surprised you aren't asking Pastor Jon to do the ceremony. After all, he is a friend to us both."

Catharine thought for a moment how to answer his question. How would he take it? "Well, there is a church policy stating pastors shouldn't marry church members to those outside their faith group."

"You're kidding! They really are exclusionists. And it's based on being part of their group rather than Christian?"

"I know how it sounds, but it has been the policy for a long time."

"I would think they'd lose converts because of it."

"I don't know, but maybe it causes some young people to think twice before jumping into a marriage with too many differences."

"I can see making it Christian, at least. But they cut the other spouse off right at the beginning or put him in a position of a forced, pretend conversion, and you know what I think of that idea." He shook his head, and Catharine felt crushed.

"If you don't mind me asking, what was your first wedding like?"

"Well, beautiful. Kenji's two sisters came from Japan. They rented a special Japanese wedding dress and brought it with them as their wedding gift. They wore gorgeous kimonos. It was in the Rose Chapel in Pasadena, and we invited friends and our whole church. We had a cake-and-punch reception and went off to the Disneyland Hotel for three days, then back to school and work."

"It sounds wonderful. We had a monstrous wedding and dinner in Philadelphia—too much money for her parents and for only a couple of hours. I'm glad I have sons."

A burning question popped into Catharine's mind. "What if you had lost your job here? Could our relationship have continued?"

"I had it all planned out if such a thing should happen. I would get a job as a high school science teacher in commuting distance. I wasn't about to let you go."

Catharine laughed and gave him a hug.

When they got to the cottage, she didn't invite him in, and he didn't ask.

She got on the phone and called Matt and Carol, giving them the good news. They expressed happiness for her. She knew they would because they had encouraged her friendship with Aaron during her Christmas visit. They wouldn't be able to come east with the baby and work responsibilities in June, but they hoped for a fall visit around Thanksgiving.

In the evening she went to visit Mama at Eden Court. She walked in with her hand outstretched. "You're wearing jewelry!" her mother said, missing the significance of the gesture. "Why are you wearing jewelry?"

"Mama, it's an engagement ring!"

"Oh, wonderful," she said and settled back. "I'm glad for you, but there's the religion thing."

"Yes, but I am fifty-three, and there won't be any problems about how to raise children, will there?"

"I guess not. I was so happy Kenji was a church member; I didn't care about his race," she said.

"Come on, Mama. I remember you saying, 'Why can't you marry an American?'"

"Did I? I don't remember. Anyway, Aaron's a wonderful man. He's always been so good to me. But didn't you explain to him that we don't wear jewelry? We give watches?"

"No, Mama, I didn't expect this. It was a surprise. Besides, things are changing in the larger denominational world around the cities, at least. Women wear small earrings and pendants hanging on chains around their necks, nothing ostentatious, simple jewelry."

"It's because worldliness is creeping in."

"Yes," laughed Catharine. "I guess they forgot the old saying: 'If it touches your skin, it's a sin, but okay if it's a pin.'"

"Umph," said Mama. "You're laughing at the old standards."

Catharine regretted mocking the old ways of her mother's era. "No, I'm really not. I respect your standards. I just have other priorities than insulting my fiancé by returning his ring. It's all about what it means to him and me; it symbolizes a relationship." She cocked her head, remembering another relationship symbol. "It's like the Sabbath."

An assistant brought in her mother's supper and gave Catharine the chance to change the subject.

She talked briefly about their wedding plans. When she left, her mother looked happy, but she expressed one parting plea. "When am I going to see my home again?"

"I don't know, Mama."

ॐ

It didn't take long for Catharine's students to notice her engagement ring and congratulate her. The girls were particularly excited and came forward to inspect it, some dreaming of the day they would wear such a romantic symbol.

Catharine continued plans for the class trip to see the Old Testament sanctuary on display at the Mennonite Visitor's Center in Lancaster. They had hoped to visit around Easter, but other parties had the same idea. She made reservations for their large group in May. Her goal wasn't just to introduce the students to a relic of Hebrew history but to show them how the Old Testament ritual played itself out in the New.

As they entered the bus on a sunny spring morning, Catharine told her students, "We are thankful the Mennonites built a copy of this 'show-and-tell' given to Israel in the wilderness. Unfortunately, most Bible students consider it an obsolete Jewish tradition and ignore its purpose of teaching Israel about the plan of salvation through a coming Messiah. As time passed, God's people lost the meaning of the service and obsessed on the material building and rituals."

When the group arrived at the Visitor's Center, a cheery, middle-aged Mennonite lady ushered them into the courtyard of the model sanctuary. She introduced herself as Jean. Her blue eyes sparkled as she explained the various symbols to the students. She smiled frequently as she related her own relationship to Christ, the Lamb. Jean told them that in today's culture she wouldn't talk so freely with other tourists, but she wanted to express her faith to the young Bible students.

They moved on to the tabernacle. "The Old Testament sanctuary is a shadow of the heavenly sanctuary in Hebrews 8:5," she said. "And the one exhibited here is a pale shadow of the ancient structure in the wilderness, where it had shone with bronze and gold, linens and animal skins, scarlet, purple, and blue trappings, richly robed priests and the High Priest, precious stones, and ornate embroidery and carvings."

As they entered the Most Holy Place, part of the tabernacle, the ark of the covenant, captured Catharine's gaze. A strange feeling came over her as the oblong box and its cherubim took on a golden glow. She felt a compulsion to open it. She knew the biblical one held the Ten Commandments. Placed separately beside them were specific laws for the primitive culture of the newly escaped slaves from Egypt. There had also been the staff of Aaron, the first High Priest, and a sample of manna. She stood transfixed for several minutes as Jean's voice drifted into the background. Then she looked around to see whether anyone else saw the "glow." Apparently not, since the students kept their eyes on the speaker, only briefly looking at the ark.

"The sanctuary was where God revealed Himself to His people, accepted, and forgave them. Today He meets us through Christ," Catharine said to get her mind off the vision. But for the rest of the day and after, she mentally questioned her own eyesight and never told anyone about the incident.

Jean presented an hour of information and history, and ended the tour with a prayer "to be moved by the Spirit and find renewed faith in this prophetic and sacred place where our spiritual ancestors met God."

"Read about it again in Exodus 25 and Hebrews 9 and 10," she said.

CHAPTER 32

Catharine and Aaron set their wedding date for the middle of June, after their last classes met and the last exams were taken. She let it be known that she wanted no gifts and would send out announcements later. Nevertheless, a few days before the wedding, Mrs. Koster planned a surprise shower at her home and invited women from the college, a few students who hadn't left for the summer, and other friends. Except for some small home appliances, it proved to be a shower of colorful negligees. She wondered how long it would take to wear them all.

Every time Catharine thought of her wedding, her heart beat faster as if it were dancing inside her rib cage. She hadn't felt so happy in years. Believing she had moved away from grief, feelings of betrayal, and questions about Kenji's love for her, she was ready to start a new life.

She needed to find closure to the mystery still stalking her and to fulfill Kenji's wish, to get his research papers into friendly hands. The local police had never found any leads on the February trashing of the cottage. Catharine thought that, not finding what they were looking for, they had given up. Yet she and Aaron would continue the search.

After a week of rain and uniformly gray skies, Catharine was pleased to see the sun shining on her wedding day.

"I think of the rain as washing away the angst of the last few months," she told Chiro.

The cat stood next to her, looking into the full-length mirror as Catharine dressed for the big moment. Always by her side, he followed her around the cottage like a gray shadow. If he were human, she would have considered him smothering. She thought of Aaron's attentiveness.

She liked her reflection, an attractive woman who looked younger than her age. She had chosen a summer dress of blue variegated flowers with a short, white linen jacket. She wore her hair down today, and its length surprised her. It had been a long time since she let it fall around her, and she remembered for an instant that Kenji had liked it down. She wondered whether it was wrong to think of her first husband on her wedding day.

"I hope Aaron also likes it down," she said to Chiro.

At one o'clock in the afternoon, she joined the Kosters and drove with them to Eden Court.

"Mama, you look lovely," said Catharine upon entering her mother's room. A woman from a nearby salon had done her hair and puffed it up to cover her scalp. She had added a bit of red tint to bring out her original color. Her mother was dressed in an ivory suit she hadn't seen before.

"Josie bought it for me," she said.

A nurse helped her into a wheelchair, and Catharine pushed her downstairs to the chapel.

Everyone was there: Debbie; Jerry; Jonas; Zach; Josie and Jake; James and his latest girlfriend; the Kosters; Kris and Erika; and Pastor Jon and his wife, Linda. Laitha and her husband, Bob, had come up from Washington with Mary Katharine. Aaron had also invited Dr. Kerry. Aaron stood at the front, handsome in his navy church suit. James and Laitha stood up with them.

Jerry was about to play his guitar and sing when the back chapel doors opened and a tall, thin woman in a purple dress with pure-white hair piled atop her head entered. She exuded elegance, and although she was probably seventy, she wore stiletto heels. Catharine turned and saw Sarah slip into a back seat.

Catharine wanted to run to her and hug her before she might slip away again, but instead she raised her arm in greeting. The distraction almost caused her to forget what she was doing, but when she locked eyes with Aaron, even Sarah faded into the background.

When the ceremony finished, they walked to the back, and Catharine grabbed Sarah around the neck. "Sarah, Sarah, you came to my wedding! I'm so glad to see you. How I've missed you."

"I've missed you too, little sister." They both stood there, crying.

Taking Aaron's hand, she brought him forward. "This is Aaron, my husband." She emphasized the word *husband*.

Then she remembered her mother. Josie pushed the wheelchair behind them. As soon as Sarah saw her, she stooped and hugged her a long time. "It's Sarah, Mama. I'm actually here."

There was much crying before Dr. Kerry appeared at the door of the chapel and announced, "Your limo is ready to leave." He wore a chauffeur's cap. "This is your wedding gift," he said, smiling broadly. They filed out to the elongated limo for the hour-long trip to dinner at the Hershey Hotel.

When the vehicle parked at the entrance, two neatly dressed assistants came to open their doors. Aaron jumped out, saying, "I'll get our bags and check in." He gazed at her for a couple of seconds as he lifted the suitcases and put them on a cart. Then he winked, pursed his lips, and strode away. Then he turned, looked back, and waved, just as he had the first day they met.

Another assistant waited with a wheelchair. "I'm here to help the young lady," he said, pointing to Mama. Very gently he helped Mama into the wheelchair and took her to the dining room, while chatting jovially.

"Mama's just drinking in all the attention," said Sarah.

Tall windows framed the spacious room, and tables had been put together for their party. Fresh yellow roses adorned each one, and white linens, luxury china, and golden utensils added to the rich display. Several beautifully wrapped packages sat on one table.

It seemed to take Aaron a long time to join them at the table, but he made a grand entrance, Catharine thought, more dressed up than she had ever seen him. She wanted to fall into his arms right there. He kissed her, and she felt his touch through her whole being.

During the meal, Sarah talked a lot and seemed happy. Many sentences began with "Do you remember when …?" Catharine felt slightly annoyed at the nostalgia trip. She was looking to the future on this special day, while Sarah was trying to make up for the past.

The brightest moment came when Catharine mentioned that she hoped her mother would be able to come home for a couple of months during the summer.

"Yes, you told me on the phone," Sarah said. "What if I came back and stayed with Mama part of the time—maybe all of it—and let you two spend your first summer finding a place or doing what you need to do?"

"Sarah, it would be wonderful. We have the cottage already, you know, and we plan to remodel the farmhouse this summer and live there part of the year."

Sarah laughed. "How exciting to keep it in the family and feel welcome to come back anytime. Call me when you get back from Canada." She sat back in her chair, smiling and relaxed.

And so did Catharine.

CHAPTER 33

After all the good-byes had been said and gifts and cards had been opened and packed to go home with Mama and Sarah, Aaron and Catharine left for their room. When they reached it, Aaron opened the door and turned toward her. "I'm going to carry you across the threshold." They both laughed as he swept her up, and they entered the room.

"Oh my," said Catharine. The soft light and fragrance coming from about a dozen lit aromatic candles filtered through the room, as did the low strains of classical music. "It's so beautiful. Did you arrange this?"

"Some of it," he said, putting her down on the bed and falling into her open arms.

∞

They slept late the next day, Monday, and toured Hershey Park.

After a late lunch, Aaron told her, "I have arranged a special spa treatment for you. How about having one of Hershey's famous chocolate massages?"

"Wow, it would be great. Don't you want one too?"

"No, I'm not much for chocolate on me, just inside me! But I'll get a regular massage at the same time."

Downstairs at the spa, an attendant rubbed Catharine with warm, thick dark unsweetened chocolate, and she lay encased in it for twenty minutes of pure relaxation. Next the attendant moved a pole above her, and warm water from large shower heads on the pole rinsed the chocolate from her body. She dried with hot, thick towels and noticed the softened and silky feel of her skin.

On Tuesday morning, she and Aaron left on a plane from Harrisburg via Philadelphia to Toronto. They walked around the clean modern city of Toronto, had dinner, and finally boarded the Rail Canada train at ten o'clock in the evening.

They climbed up into a prepared berth; it was cozy but wide enough for both of them. Sheets of pastel pink felt soft against their bodies as they prepared for bed.

By the next morning, the train had entered an area so remote that not a building or town could be glimpsed on the horizon. The train sped through this vast forested landscape all day. They saw hundreds of lakes scattered along the route, and occasionally the train stopped while a group of men alighted with their fishing gear.

"I've got to go fishing here someday," Aaron said.

They spent most of the day in the windowed lounge, viewing the passing scenery. On the third day the train reached the prairie and farmlands of Central Canada, and its passengers enjoyed a spectacular sunset.

"Years ago we traveled to Western Canada from California," Catharine said. "I saw the most beautiful scenery in my life. I love mountains and even prefer the rugged Canadian Rockies to my ancestors' Switzerland."

They arrived at Edmonton early on the fourth day and rented a car near the station.

After breakfast they found the B&B where Aaron had made reservations. "This city is easy to get around in," he said.

They found no listing of a Yamashiro or a Mae Yoder in the phonebook. In the afternoon Catharine and Aaron went online to find the Mennonite churches in the area. "Hey," he said, "The first Mennonites came to Canada from Pennsylvania in 1789." They found about half a dozen churches in the city.

They went down the list of churches in the area and called each to inquire whether they had a member with the first name of Mae, possibly Yoder or even Yamashiro. None of them did. The closest they came was an Ella Mae at a church in another town. There were different types of Mennonite churches. Catharine's family and the Yoders belonged to an Old Order Mennonite group that still practiced shunning. She didn't think Mae would continue as part of the conservative group. Maybe she'd left the church entirely or became something else, as Catharine's father had.

The first Sunday they attended a Sunday school in one church and the worship service in another. During the week they visited the offices of larger churches.

"Our time in Edmonton ends next week, and then we continue to Vancouver on the train," Catharine reminded her husband. "We have only one more Sunday to look at outlying churches."

"We can do more sight-seeing, I hope," said Aaron.

Clarkston, a small town twenty minutes from Edmonton, was their last church visit. The Clarkston Sunday school was less interesting than the one in the city. They introduced themselves and asked about Mae Yoder with no result. Then they climbed the stairs to the sanctuary for the church service. A typical Protestant program had begun. "I see only two head scarves, and the women wear jewelry and modern dress," Catharine noted. Music played, and people sang while the couple walked to the front and found seats on the right side.

Before the sermon, Catharine noticed a violin solo listed in the program to be given by Dr. Darian Overholt. The announcer introduced him as a local physician. As Dr. Overholt walked across the platform, Catharine fainted.

CHAPTER 34

As Catharine gained awareness, Aaron cradled her in his arms, and she looked up into the face of a young Kenji. People around them were stirring and whispering.

"I'm Dr. Overholt," the twin Kenji said. "I think we should get you out into the open air."

The two men, one on each side, escorted her to a side door. Once outside, the doctor took her pulse and did a quick examination. "Let me get my stethoscope," he said.

"It won't be necessary," said Aaron. "She just had a very big shock."

"What do you mean?" Dr. Overholt said.

"It's you," Aaron said. "Is your mother's name Mae Yoder?"

"Yoder is her maiden name. Why?"

"And your father's name?"

"It was Yamashiro, but I never knew him. What's this all about?"

"We had better introduce ourselves. I am Aaron Zadlo, and this is my wife, Catharine, the former Mrs. Yamashiro."

Catharine finally managed to speak. "You look almost exactly like Kenji when he was young. I am his widow. He died two and half years ago."

The news hung in the air while the young man stepped back and put his hand behind his neck. Then he said, "He's dead?" She thought he looked as if he could cry. "I don't know what to say. This is a shock. I often think of him and wonder what happened to him."

He continued, "Why are you contacting me now? I wanted to know him alive."

"We didn't even know you existed," said Aaron. "We came here, looking for your mother, to see if Kenji may have given her some important papers."

"Let me find my wife, and we'll take you to our house. Wait here. Oh, and I'll see if I can find my parents too." He looked flustered.

"You'd better sit down, Mrs. Yamashiro. I mean—I don't remember your name," he said, turning to Aaron.

"Aaron Zadlo."

Dr. Overholt led them to a bench nearby.

When Darian Overholt returned, a young Asian woman and a couple, who were about Catharine's age, followed him. Then he introduced everyone. His wife was Gloria; his step-father, John; and his mother, Mae. He asked the newcomers to call him Darian. Mae Overholt came over and gave the still-stunned Catharine a hug.

"We're going to have a lot of catching up to do," she said.

Darian went to get the car.

Aaron broke an awkward silence. "We just got married Sunday, two weeks ago."

"Congratulations!" each one said.

Darian drove up in a new Sierra Camry, and the group got in. Darian carefully helped Catharine into a backseat with Aaron as if she were elderly, fragile, or both. Maybe it was because her hands were still shaking.

They drove down the road to a semirural area and turned left on a private road, ending at a brick rancher with a horse barn behind it. The yard was vast and manicured with colorful flowers in front of the house.

They hadn't driven far, and apparently plans had been made for Sunday dinner, as the smell of roasting chicken filled the front room. "You will have dinner with us, of course," said Gloria.

"Well, thank you, Gloria. We don't want to inconvenience you. You weren't expecting extra company, I'm sure," Catharine said.

"We have plenty, and you're welcome."

Gloria added two extra places at the large table and came to sit in the living room with the rest of them.

"I know we all have lots of questions," Mae said. "So I'll get started." She proved to be a cheerful, outspoken woman who smiled a lot. Slightly overweight and short, she still looked young and attractive with dark-blonde hair. She put them all at ease in the awkward situation.

"I've been here since 1970, when I came to live with an elderly aunt and uncle who have since died. But I have cousins—first, second, and third cousins. We have a large extended family here, and they have no contact with those left in Pennsylvania. It seemed like the perfect place to hide. The Yoders in Pennsylvania are Old Order Mennonites, and the Yoders who came here are liberal and were shunned by the ones who stayed. I knew I would be shunned, so I never returned. After a month I called my mother, Rachel, to let her know I was going to join another church. That put the lid on my coffin, and I never told them about Darian. My annulment was final, I remarried two years later, and John legally adopted Darian. My family here has been accepting and caring. I'm thankful every day for them. Well," she said, pausing, "you have my story. Now, tell me what happened to Kenji."

Catharine sat up straight and led them through her meeting with Kenji at church, at school, and then in California. "We both attended graduate school in Pasadena. I went to Fuller Seminary, and he went to the Pasadena Institute of Technology. The first six months I had a room in someone's house, and he had a studio apartment in the back yard. We married six months later and found a place in an apartment complex, where we lived for years and worked part time. After getting our degrees, we taught full-time. Our son, Matt, was born, and we found a house. Kenji was invited to come to Washington, DC, to work at the Physics Institute, and I taught at area colleges until a position opened up at a Methodist seminary. In January 2005, at age fifty-five, Kenji seeming in the best of health went running in cold weather and had a heart attack."

Many questions came from both sides after their stories concluded. By then Gloria had dinner ready.

Later in the day, Catharine took Mae aside and asked her the burning question that had been running through her mind all day. "I need to know. Did Kenji visit you here two years ago? And did he give you some papers?"

"I never saw my husband again," she said. "No, he never came to see me."

Catharine noticed Mae cross her arms and look uncomfortable for the first time since they had met. Catharine didn't believe her and asked the question a different way. "Did you know he was here?"

"I did know he was in town. But he talked to one of my cousins, who was visiting his mother at the time. He's a lawyer and advised Kenji not to make contact before some things could be worked out," said Mae. "Kenji heard about Darian for the first time from my cousin before he made the trip."

Darian came behind her and heard the last part of the conversation. "He was so wrong!" he said. Head down, he punched the back of the chair nearest him and started to sob. "If only I had taken the time to look for him! I thought he knew about me and didn't care!"

Mae retrieved a tissue and gave it to him. "I thought the news would have drifted down to Pennsylvania from someone up here," she said. "But apparently it didn't. So my mother doesn't know about her grandson."

Catharine said, "I talked to her daughter, Anna, and I'm sure she doesn't know. She only told me about the marriage."

Mae looked off into space and said slowly, "My dear sister, Anna. How is she?"

"She seems to be doing fine; she's married to a farmer and has a daughter, Esther, who is one of my students at the Midland Bible College."

"Yes, I did hear she had married Cecil Yoder and had two children," Mae said. "Getting back to Kenji, my cousin said he planned to come back and bring you, Catharine. What were the papers you asked about?"

"They were research papers. I think we need to contact your cousin."

"I'm afraid it would be impossible. He died of a heart attack last spring. He didn't live here and was visiting his parents when Kenji saw him. He lived in Maryland."

Catharine squinted, then opened her eyes wide, looking hard at Mae. "What was his name?"

"Miles Pollack," she said.

Chapter 35

Catharine's first reaction to the news of Miles Pollack in Edmonton came from inside, a heart palpitation, a few butterflies hatching in her stomach, but she determined not to let them escape. *Just stay nonchalant and let the plot unfold*, she told herself.

"How interesting," Catharine said upon hearing Pollack's name. "He was Kenji's lawyer in Washington, DC, though I never met him. Apparently he was helping Kenji with some issues at the Physics Institute, where he worked."

"Wow!" said Mae. "I wonder how they met."

"A good question," said Catharine.

"But we still need to contact his family," Aaron said. "Perhaps he left the papers with them. Wouldn't it make sense?"

The Pollacks lived on a farm outside town with their other son and his family. Mae accompanied Catharine and Aaron to their residence. The elderly Pollacks were the only ones at home when they arrived at the long, one-story white ranch house. Carrying on a conversation with them proved to be a challenge; both were extremely hard of hearing in spite of hearing aids.

The trip turned out to be a dead end, as the two seniors denied being given anything even remotely, such as business papers by their visiting son. Talking about her deceased son caused Mrs. Pollack to weep.

"Yes, we remember Dr. Yamashiro," said the old man. "What a kind and intelligent man he was. We're sorry to hear he is no longer with us."

After searching a large wooden desk in the living room, Mae promised to return when the rest of the family was home and go through the house. She did call Bruce, her cousin, at work to question him. He denied any knowledge of his brother leaving materials at their home. He gave Mae permission to check his brother's room, which she did and found nothing. He also told her Miles had made the two-week trip alone, and Kenji had come to the farm a week later. They had clearly known each other from Maryland.

With just two days before leaving for Vancouver, Darian invited them for one more dinner, and they freely discussed the mystery with no solutions. Catharine and Aaron gave Darian and Gloria and John and Mae a standing invitation to visit them in Pennsylvania.

"You'll see the land of your ancestors," said Mae. "Do they still have the tabernacle at the Mennonite Visitor's Center? It made a real impression on me. A church here has a smaller version, or at least they did. Actually, it's an Adventist church."

"They sure do, and I took one of my classes on a field trip there this spring," said Catharine. "Yes, I'm not surprised an Adventist church would have one. It's an important doctrine to them."

Turning to Darian, she said, "I want to give you some souvenirs of your father. I hope you'll plan a trip soon." Catharine was crying now.

"I will," the young man said. "I want to meet my brother someday, too." When he hugged her, there were tears in his eyes.

✦

Catharine sat in the dome car while Aaron went to get a drink of water. The Canadian Rockies came into view 140 miles southwest of Edmonton, and the train entered picturesque scenes worthy of paradise. They came so close to a magnificent waterfall that it sprayed the train's windows. The remoteness of the lakes, forests, and mountains gave Catharine a feeling of sacred seclusion.

She understood why Kenji had taken this train. They both felt closest to God in nature, and it had given him time to prayerfully contemplate the news of his son and how it might affect their lives. She longed for the spiritual bond they had once shared. *He will always be in my heart, and I'll love him forever.*

Maybe it was because of her Swiss roots, but mountains reflected a spiritual and timeless beauty; their snow-covered rocks, a solid, immovable foundation, reaching up to God through all sorts of weather. When life seemed shaky, it was comforting to remember the mountains in Yosemite, Switzerland, and now the Rockies.

At the end of the train trip, Catharine and Aaron discovered the uniqueness of Vancouver, the Englishness of Victoria, and the beauty of Butchart Gardens before they boarded the plane for Washington.

Settling back in the coach seat, Catharine said, "Shall we look for Kushner while in Washington or go home and get some rest?"

"Rest? The farmhouse needs big-time cleaning and dusting from sitting empty all winter. We need to get back to Chiro and Logan. They'll think they've been abandoned and given away to strangers."

Catharine sighed. "I've lost my connection to Kushner with Marti gone. Even if we locate him on the Internet, we can't just show up at his house—if he's still in Washington. With the excitement of getting married and the trip over, we had better get to work!"

"Come on, there'll be lots more excitement for us." Aaron laughed, grabbed her, and gave her a passionate kiss, causing smiles from the people across the aisle.

"I mean," she said, straightening her clothes, "we must face the reality of possible future threats from Kushner and find him before something else happens."

"And what will we do when we find him? We can't prove anything."

"We can confront him and ask for explanations."

"Which he will deny."

CHAPTER 36

Since the move to Eden Court, Catharine experienced time spent with her mother as often tedious. It swallowed up hours when she needed to study for class. Catharine felt guilty about these coldhearted thoughts. The dutiful visits, the attempts at cheerfulness, old sitcom reruns, and complaints repeated so many times, she was unable to focus on them. Worst of all, she thought her mother could see through her pretense.

Yet she loved this woman with all her being and remembered her as hardworking and loving. It hurt to see Mama trapped in a body she couldn't move more than a few yards using a walker. With skin so wrinkled and thin, blue veins showed through; no longer a barrier against injury, her skin bruised at the slightest mishap. All these things pulled at Catharine's heart as she went to her mother's side at Eden Court the day after returning from Canada.

How much do I tell her about the trip, about Mae, about Darian? Or are these secrets she should never hear?

"Hello, Mama," she said while giving her a tight hug.

"Mind that shoulder," she said. "It hasn't changed."

After showing pictures of the trip and wedding photos from

the Eden Court chapel ceremony, Catharine gave her mother a limited travelogue of the trip. Then she described her plans to clean the house.

"Mama, do you mind if we go through some things and straighten up the house a bit?"

"As long as you don't put things where I can't find them," she said.

She still thinks she's coming home!

Catharine's spirit broke a little, but then suddenly she came to life. "Hey, Mama, what if, after we finish getting the house in order, we bring you home for the summer while I'm not working?"

Without thinking, she had blurted it out and regretted the impulsive words.

Her mother's face was wreathed in a smile; her tired eyes opened up as she raised the wrinkles on her forehead. "Oh, honey, could I?"

"I'll see how everything goes. First you'll need to be up to it physically, so stay healthy in the next couple of weeks, Mama."

"I will! I will!"

Now I will need to convince Aaron of this.

❦

Catharine and Aaron stayed at the cottage while tackling the cleanup of the farmhouse. Jerry had kept the mowing up for the season, so they started inside the house. Catharine found it fulfilling to see changes occur and the rooms brighten. They came home bone weary each weekday. The house hadn't seen such a thorough cleaning and painting in decades.

"It's like a baptism," she told Aaron. "You clean out the dirt and dust of the house but leave all the good things and memories."

Aaron looked up, and their eyes locked. "You've forgiven him?"

"Oh, yes, yes." She ran to him, and they embraced.

⟡

It took two weeks instead of one to have the house move-in ready. Catharine looked forward to going through her parents' old souvenirs and papers. *What secrets will they give up?*

While Aaron painted and repaired, Catharine went through old family records. She found yellowed business papers and farm receipts from thirty years ago and shredded them. Important documents, such as her parents' wedding certificate, she carefully protected with acid-free paper and stored them in a labeled metal box. *How interesting. They got married in Ellicott City, Maryland.*

Among the documents was a birth and death certificate for Rachel Brubaker Weaver. At age twelve, Mama had told Catharine about a sister who died as a baby of something called SIDS. She'd first heard the name from a visiting aunt who said Catharine looked like Rachel. Not knowing about Rachel then, she'd puzzled over who she might be. Those were the only times Rachel's name was uttered until Mama talked about her at Eden Court. Catharine showed the certificates to Aaron and put them with the other protected documents. *My poor sister never had a chance to live. What would she have been like?*

On her next visit to Eden Court, she noticed a memory lapse when she told Mama she'd found Rachel's birth record. "Why, Rachel was your sister. Didn't I tell you?" She put her hand to her head. "Daddy never allowed us to say her name because of Sarah."

"Yes, you told me about it."

Her mother screwed up her face, as if trying to get weakening brain cells to recall what she was going to say. "I can't remember," she said, throwing up her lower arms.

184

"It's all right, Mama. You don't need to remember."

When Catharine left Eden Court, she decided to call Sarah.

∂♫♪

"Hello, Sarah. It's Catharine."

"Is something wrong?" She sounded alarmed over the phone. "Is Mama okay?"

"Yes, Sarah, she is. I've been thinking about what we said at the dinner about bringing her home for the summer. What do you think?"

"Oh, Catharine, I'm so glad. I mean, of course it would be great for her." She sounded relieved. Catharine waited for her to continue.

She's not mentioning her promise to stay at the farmhouse and help Mama. Does she have early dementia or just want to get out of it?

Sarah congratulated her again on her marriage and asked about the trip—*As if it was a duty,* thought Catharine.

After giving a brief description of what they'd seen, Catharine said, "I have something else to ask you, Sarah. What do you remember about Rachel? I found her birth certificate while organizing things at the house. Mama said you took it hard."

Sobbing followed a long silence.

"Sarah, what's wrong?"

"I can't talk about it." More sobbing. "Please, Catharine, it was a bad time. Please don't bring it up again." The phone went dead.

"Wow, how harsh," Catharine said to the air.

About an hour later, Sarah called back.

"I need to apologize. Of course, you never knew Rachel. I'm sorry to have been so rude. I just loved her a lot, then she was gone. I missed her; that's all."

Sarah choked on the last two words, and Catharine wondered if missing Rachel really was all that was bothering her sister.

"Of course, Sarah, I understand. It must have been hard for you to lose her."

Catharine expressed empathy while at the same time wondering why Sarah had been so distant and teased *her* as a child. Catharine realized how little she knew about her sister; she was a stranger, as was the faceless George, her son, whom she hadn't seen since he was a child.

Do I dare bring up the promise to come and stay with Mama?, she wondered.

She decided to jump into it. "Sarah, at our wedding dinner, you mentioned the possibility of coming up to stay with Mama this summer. Would Vince let you be away so long?"

"Vince isn't living with me now, Catharine."

"Oh no. I'm sorry, Sarah."

"It's okay to talk about it. I guess I should have told you when I was up there, but I didn't want to spoil the fun. And like I told you, George is living in Texas with his wife and three kids. He has Vince and his relatives there. I guess I'm a bit lonely, and, yes, I will come for two months. Let me know when you want me; I'm free anytime."

Her tone had changed dramatically from the first call. Catharine could only say, "We would all appreciate having you here, and I need to get to know you again, don't I?"

Sarah said something very strange. "Maybe you won't like me."

Chapter 37

"Mama, the house is ready for you," Catharine said as she burst into her mother's room at Eden Court on July 15. Mama was already waiting in a wheelchair.

"What a smile," said Aaron, coming in behind her. "I've never seen you light up like this." He gave her a hug and said, "All these suitcases ready to go?"

⁂

When they arrived home, the delight on Catharine's mother's face radiated through the house.

"For a week we are going to be your constant company, so you'd better get used to us," Catharine told her. "You can use a walker now and go anywhere you like with one of us."

"Whata ya say, Mama? What about a trip up over the mountains to State College for lunch tomorrow?" said Aaron.

"We'll see how I'm doing in the morning," she said. "Are you going somewhere after a week?" Catharine was surprised at her sharpness in picking up the inference.

"Yes, we're planning a trip to Washington, and someone is

going to be here to watch out for you." She saw Mama's eyes cloud up, and the wrinkles between them get deeper.

"Don't worry. I guarantee you will like this caregiver."

Mama put her hands behind her ears, trying to catch the sound waves. "And who would that be, may I ask?"

"Guess, Mama. Who loves you as much as me?"

"Is it Sarah?" She left her mouth open, waiting.

"Yes, it's Sarah." And they hugged while Mama chuckled.

Her mother went around the house, moving the walker ahead and then pulling her body forward, touching walls, furniture, everything, as if welcoming long-lost friends; or were they welcoming her? She came to the kitchen pantry where she fumbled around, picking up cans and holding them close to her eyes. "Who mixed up my pantry? Nothing's in its right place!"

"Well, I did," said Catharine. "I tried to put similar things together and make it more organized." She felt a tiny twinge of agitation at the question.

"My dear Catharine, for someone so smart, you don't think. I had them all where I could find them because my eyesight is so poor. I go by feeling."

"I'm sorry, Mama. You're right, and you've told me before. Well, after you rest, you can show me where things go, and we'll rearrange them so you can find them."

A week later Sarah arrived at Jacob's Farm in her BMW. She had driven alone all the way from Florida. Catharine had suggested that she fly, but Sarah had wanted to make it a vacation trip. "I found the neatest B&Bs all the way. I had them all mapped out and reserved. The most annoying part was getting out of Florida. It's such a long state; you feel like you're not making progress."

Sarah moved into the newly decorated room Rose had once used. Catharine decorated it with a lavender-and-purple theme,

Sarah's favorite colors. She set family photos around and provided fresh flowers. Catharine beamed when Sarah said, "It's so beautiful. You always were good at decorating."

It was a time of celebration, and they invited all the local people who had attended the wedding and then some.

✑

On a weekday evening Catharine and Aaron went out to dinner at an elegant restaurant in Harrisburg to plan their trip to Washington.

Catharine noticed a familiar face from the side a couple of tables away. She tried to remember who it was. "Aaron, do you recognize that woman over there in the green outfit?"

"No, can't say I do. No one from the college. Maybe your church?"

"Hey, she looks a lot like Marvina Brown, Ralph's mother. But she's dressed up and has lost a few pounds." The woman wore a stylish pantsuit, matching green earrings, and a large necklace. Her hair was dyed a dark brown, almost black. Marvina had mostly gray hair.

"Are you sure? You're describing a big change."

"Don't stare. I have a feeling I shouldn't let her know I'm here." Catharine carefully moved her chair behind a large plant.

She also noticed that the woman sat with an equally well-dressed man in a business suit. And she had to wonder, *Is this really Marvina Brown? Perhaps I'm mistaken, or has Marvina come into some money?*

The incident reminded Catharine to call Marvina and check on Ralph to see how he was doing. She called the next day.

"Why, he's as good as gold," Marvina said. "No problems as long as he keeps medicating. But without it he goes wild."

"What does *wild* mean?"

"He hallucinates," she said. "See's things like men dressed in black or witches or something. He tells me they scare him. But rest assured, he only had it happen once since we saw you. He takes his medicine regularly."

"I planned to call you before this," Catharine said. "Were you home yesterday?"

"Yeah, just went to the grocery store," she said.

I am either mistaken, or she's hiding something.

⁂

On a Thursday, Catharine and Aaron drove to Washington in the Camry and stayed at a B&B she remembered outside town. They planned to visit the institute first and see Laitha the following week.

After waiting out a morning thunderstorm, they drove to the Physics Institute on Friday. The weather reminded her of why she disliked Washington summers. The heavy, moist air pressed their bodies like an invisible, clammy glove. The Physics Institute offices looked transformed when they walked in. The attractive young woman seemed more in keeping with her modernized surroundings than the older woman she had replaced.

It was lunchtime, and while waiting for the platinum-blonde receptionist to get off the phone, she saw three men and a woman walk through the reception area. Catharine didn't recognize any of them. Then her husband's old friend Victor Hammond came out of an office. He had been a colleague Kenji hung out with, playing tennis and golf and just talking. He seemed older now, balding, with a brooding look on his round face. But still the tanned athlete, he walked briskly with an aura of confidence.

She greeted him. "Hello, Victor." He stopped, and there was an awkward second, when she didn't think he remembered her. "I'm Catharine. I was Kenji Yamashiro's wife." She looked into his dark eyes, which reminded her of black buttons on a stuffed doll.

He shook her hand. "Of course, I remember you." *Was it her imagination, or did a troubled look come over his already sullen countenance?* "It's been a while. What brings you here?"

"This is my husband, Aaron Zadlo." The two men shook hands. "While in Washington, I wanted to say hello to Dr. Kushner. I understand he's retired."

"Yes, it's been about a year now. He was replaced by John Lager. You remember him?"

"I do. Where is Dr. Kushner now? Is he in the area?"

"I believe he lives somewhere in the South. Too far away to visit, I'm sure."

"Did he move to Florida?"

"Could be. I don't know. I have heard he has had some health problems."

"Is there anyone else here I might know?" Catharine said.

"I don't think so. It's only me and John from the old days."

How strange, she thought, *that so many people left. Even the receptionist.*

"Well, I had better be on my way. It's good to see you again, Catharine, and to meet your husband. Have a good trip."

A nameplate on the desk identified the shapely receptionist as Kim Fox. "Miss Fox, would you have an address and phone number for Dr. Raymond Kushner, the former director?" Catharine said. "He was a colleague of my husband when he worked here three years ago. I would like to visit him."

"I wouldn't normally give it out, but I see you know Victor, and he is the associate director, so I'll get it for you." She turned to her computer, and in a short time she printed out the information and gave it to them. The address was in Virginia, in Warrenton, a wealthy Washington suburb below the Beltway. *Not more than a daily commute.*

CHAPTER 38

On Sunday they followed their GPS to a multicolumned colonial house sitting back from the road in a residential district. Climbing the steps of the prominent front porch and going to a heavy oak door, Aaron lifted the ornate metal knocker. He didn't need to knock; it played a tune upon his lifting it. The tune triggered a voice requesting to know their business.

"We have come to see Dr. Kushner," Catharine said, a little too loud. "I knew him before he retired."

"I'm sorry he's not here," the female voice said. "It's Sunday morning, and he's at church."

Catharine looked at Aaron with her mouth open. "Impossible," she said. "He's an atheist."

The door flew open, and a Hispanic woman wearing a blue apron faced them, smiling widely. "Well, he isn't now. Praise the Lord!"

The exuberant woman invited them in. "I'm Delores. He should be home soon. I'm sure he'll want to talk to you. Can I get you something to drink?"

"No, we're fine," said Aaron.

They waited in a large parlor with lush carpets, two couches, and walls filled with eighteenth-century paintings. Catharine reflected on what she had just heard. About thirty minutes later, Dr. Kushner entered alone. He looked older than she remembered; he was also thinner but not thin. A tan, a red bulbous nose, and a face marked with age spots inferred he liked golfing or some other sun sport.

"I was at the Presbyterian church up the street," he said. "Great place." His accent didn't fit the Presbyterian church. It was clearly northeastern Jewish.

"What can I do for you?" He looked at Catharine, and sudden recognition came. "You're Kenji's wife!"

Lunging at her, he encircled her with his long arms, and blurted, "I'm so glad I got to see you again. I'm so sorry for the way I treated Kenji." The man was audibly crying. He let her go. "Delores," he yelled, "get me some Kleenex." The Hispanic woman came running with a box of tissues.

Catharine recalled the cold reception she'd received from him at the San Diego conference years ago. After he got his composure back, Catharine said to him, "Of course, I forgive you. Are you a Christian now, Dr. Kushner?"

"Please call me Ray."

She introduced Aaron at this point.

"I'm a work in progress, the pastor says. At least I don't hate them anymore." He laughed while dabbing his eyes from crying a minute ago.

"I don't know if you heard my wife is gone. Muriel got killed in a shooting accident more than a year ago. We went hunting—I used to like hunting and guns. She didn't. I talked her into going this one time. My hunting buddy, Ted, couldn't make it.

"She was a Christian, and I made fun of her like I did Kenji." He blew his nose again with a snort. "It was my fault. She picked up my gun, and it went off at close range. She didn't think it was loaded, because we were just getting out of the car."

Catharine took his arm to console him. "You don't need to talk about it."

But he continued. "I got myself in a black hole and tried suicide but couldn't do it. The chaplain from her church saw me through it. I knew what I had to do: change my life for her and stop hating myself and everybody else.

"The chaplain got me started tutoring kids and talked religious stuff. He called it spiritual direction. I even read the Bible. Funny how those crazy stories from childhood make sense when you learn what they mean, instead of carping on whether they happened or not."

"It's something a lot of people never learn," said Catharine.

"Tell me about you two. How did you meet? Where are you teaching, Catharine?"

After talking about her move to Midland Bible College, Catharine thought it was time to ask about Kenji's research.

"Ray, do you know what Kenji was working on when he died?"

"If you're talking about his space-time theory, yes and no. He thought it would make a difference in how we date organic matter. After he died, I tried for more than a year to locate his research but gave up. Now it doesn't make any difference."

"Who else knew about the research?"

"John and Victor both did. They thought the whole idea was a symptom of his religious fundamentalism, and he was trying to prove the impossible. I doubt they even looked at the research after I panned it.

"John wanted to start over with the institute—get some new younger blood. I know he wanted me to retire. When Muriel died, he said I was no use to them, too emotional."

"You said you tried to find the research. Did you ever send anyone to Pennsylvania where I live to find it?"

"No, I didn't. Maybe Lager did, but it doesn't sound like something he'd do, but he did want to destroy it. I asked Marti to look for it, and he resented it. He probably didn't try very hard."

"Have you ever heard of an attorney in the area named Miles Pollack?"

"No, can't say that I have. I wouldn't be surprised if Kenji did hire a lawyer in case his work got stolen."

"Did you give up believing in evolution?" Aaron asked.

"Not really. I'm just saying it doesn't make any difference to me. I did read a lot of Polkinghorne's stuff, and it made sense. What is faith? It's about things unseen and unknown. I've given up trying to find all the answers in my old age.

"I don't have patience with people who think my destiny depends on whether or not I accept a literal biblical interpretation of Genesis. Truth comes in all forms: myth, story, what have you. Are you saved by knowledge?"

❧

They made plans to meet with Ray Kushner before leaving Washington and going to dinner at his favorite restaurant. By the time they got to their B&B, it was almost dinnertime, and their host directed them to a vegetarian restaurant.

"We'll also have vegetarian Indian food tomorrow when we see Laitha and Bob."

Confronting John Lager came next on their itinerary. He wasn't available the next day or the next.

On the third day, Catharine convinced her husband to let her go to the Physics Institute alone. She took the metro, got off at DuPont Circle, and headed to the building where the institute occupied a whole floor. When she got off the elevator, there was John Lager coming out of the Physics Institute office. "John, I need to talk to you," she said.

He didn't look happy. "Mrs. Yamashiro, please. I'm in a hurry."

"That's not my name anymore," she said. "You used to call me Catharine, remember?"

She followed him down the hall, walking briskly.

"Look, Catharine, why are you following me? What do you want?"

"I want to know about Kenji's research papers on time theory, and you know it. I know you've been trying to get them, and you even trashed my home or sent someone to do it."

He stopped and looked at her with fire in his eyes. "Woman, you're crazy! What would I want with his hairbrained ideas? The Physics Institute would be humiliated because he worked here. If you don't stop calling and harassing me, I will notify the police!" His face had turned red, and he gritted his teeth. After throwing an obscenity from his twisted mouth, he said, "Leave me alone." He stomped off.

When she told Aaron about the incident, he slammed his right fist into his left hand and said, "I knew I should have been there."

"I don't believe I'll be going back to the institute," Catharine said.

Before leaving Washington, they fulfilled their dinner engagement with Ray Kushner. He insisted on taking them to a pricey restaurant in town.

During the meal, they asked more questions about Kenji's research and why it hadn't been taken seriously.

"I talked to him about it and briefly looked over his material. It had some validity, but I wasn't about to let him present it anywhere with our name attached, let alone publish it. He made many valuable contributions during his time with us and would have been my chosen replacement. But after this research, we felt he would make us look foolish. He had an agenda. Lager used this to undermine him. His passing was a shock."

"And the institute didn't have an agenda?" said Catharine. He ignored the question.

"I'm almost eighty years old. I stayed longer than Lager wanted. I heard from a former employee that he let three old guys go and picked up four youngsters."

"But Victor Hammond is still there."

"Yes, the only one. He has the same ideology as Lager. I did too, and we made it difficult for Kenji."

"Victor told us you were ill and lived in the south, maybe Florida."

Kushner stared at her, his bushy gray brows raised in a questioning fashion. "He knows better than that. I've lived here for thirty years! I talked to him less than a year ago. As far as I know, I'm in pretty good health."

CHAPTER 39

"The one person we have not talked to is Mrs. Miles Pollack," announced Catharine on Wednesday. "Perhaps it's time to stop at his former office and ask about her."

Before noon they located the law offices of Lane & Bergan in Bethesda on the third floor of a modest office complex. Catharine introduced herself as the widow of Miles Pollack's client, Dr. Kenji Yamashiro. The cordial receptionist searched her computer for records of two to three years ago, showing that Kenji had consulted him concerning his work at the Physics Institute. "It looks like only one consult," she said.

"He also saw him outside the office. They were business friends. Is it possible for you to give me his wife's contact information?"

"I can call her and ask if she wants to talk to you," she said.

"She wouldn't know me by name, since I never met her. I suppose I could talk to her from here."

The receptionist got Noelle Pollack on the phone, and after a brief explanation, the receptionist handed the phone to Catharine, who took it and sat on one of two couches provided in the waiting room.

"Hello, Mrs. Pollack. My name is Catharine. My deceased husband was a client of your husband. I am searching for some valuable papers he may have given to Mr. Pollack. My husband was Kenji Yamashiro. Do you recognize the name?"

"Yes, I met him when he came here to talk to Miles, a very nice man." She added soulfully, "Now they're both gone. But anything he gave him would be at his old office."

"The only thing recorded is one visit. But he consulted with your husband outside the office. They also met at his home near Edmonton, Alberta," said Catharine.

"My husband's parents live there, but I don't know anything about them meeting in Canada."

"He was there in the fall of 2004, and they met at Miles's parents' home and discussed how to protect Kenji's research records from being stolen," said Catharine. "Now I'm trying to find those papers. I have a letter saying your husband knew where they were stored. I was hoping you could help."

"I wish I could, but I don't know anything about them. It was in November when Kenji was here, after Miles's visit to Canada. From a few words I overheard, there was some sort of family situation involved."

"Really? But you don't know what it was?"

"No. Like I said, it was only a word or two about finding a family member."

"Mrs. Pollack, how did your husband die?"

"He had a heart attack. He suffered from a congenital heart condition all his life. We are glad he lasted as long as he did."

In a sympathetic tone, Catharine said, "I am glad he did too. I hope you didn't mind my questions. You have helped. I do have a favor to ask. If you have a safe or other place you put valuables, would you please check it and let me know should you find anything like research papers or even a key to a safety deposit box? I will give you my contact information."

ঔ৵

After visiting Laitha and Bob in the evening and a cousin on Thursday, they returned to the cottage late. Now that the trip to Washington was over and they were back in Pennsylvania, they had no proof that anyone from Physics Institute had broken into the cottage. There was no evidence anyone caused three heart attacks among the major players in the mystery. They had no research papers, and every route to find them was a dead end. They were no further along in finding who could be responsible for Catharine's harassment than when it had started. Were there really research papers on a vitally important project?

Catharine called Sarah and talked with Mama on Friday morning. *At least something is going right*, she thought. To her joy, the two were spending quality time together.

"I'm going to take Mama to a play on Sunday at State College. You want to go with us?" Sarah said.

Catharine declined the invitation, saying she needed to work on the women's devotional book due at the end of the summer. They made plans to meet at church the next day and have lunch at the farmhouse.

ঔ৵

On Sunday evening, at about dusk at the cottage, Catharine sat at her computer, composing, while Aaron fixed a light supper. Logan rested peacefully in his cushy homemade bed. Chiro, who had gotten used to Logan but still avoided him, lay on the floor near Catharine.

The push-out windows in front of her stood partially open, and cool night air drifted in. The air may have caused a sheet of paper to fly off the desk, and it sailed down to the floor. Catharine stooped to pick it up. As her hand touched the paper, an explosion shattered the window. She screamed, jumped to the floor, and rolled under the desk.

She thought she heard footsteps retreating outside. Aaron shouted, "Are you hurt?"

"No, I'm okay. What was it?"

"A gunshot." He grabbed something from a kitchen drawer and dashed out the front door, yelling, "Cat, call 9-1-1."

Aaron didn't want Logan shot, so he closed the door with his foot but not soon enough. The wolf dog pushed it open and lunged outside. As Aaron ran after a fleeing figure, dressed in black with what looked like a cape sailing behind him, Logan catapulted himself in a different direction, into the woods.

Grabbing the phone on the way to the door, Catharine punched 9-1-1. "Send the police right away to the Koster cottage. Someone shot out our window and barely missed me. Oh! I hear shots again. Let me see if my husband's okay." Aaron was at the door. "He is," she said and hung up.

"I saw someone running away, wearing a black cape," Aaron said. "I fired two shots in his direction to scare him."

"You have a gun?" Catharine was too shaky to scold him and let it pass.

Zeph was there in fifteen minutes, siren blaring all the way up the road. "We've got him," he said, leaping out of the car. "You both okay?"

"Yes. Who have you got?" said Catharine, anxiety in her eyes.

"Ralph Brown, of course. My men are taking him to jail right now. He was running for his life down Thirty-Five in a crazy, black outfit with a cape."

Upon entering the house, Zeph remarked on the broken glass and screen. "It's sure a good thing no one was at the desk. They'd be a goner."

Catharine's kept her face stoic, saying calmly. "I *was* at the desk. My angel was on duty because I leaned over to pick up a piece of paper. Then I heard the blast."

"Wow!"

They moved outside again. Zeph got his flashlight from the car. "Brown didn't have a weapon on him. I'm gonna look around."

He searched the yard until he found a shotgun in a patch of wet grass and carefully wrapped it in plastic with gloved hands. "Well, now we know for sure who's been after you, Catharine. You can relax now."

I'm not so sure, she thought.

"Arf, arf, arf" had been sounding in the distance. Being too shaken and distracted, no one noticed it until Aaron said, "That's Logan."

With his gun in one hand and a flashlight in the other, he bolted across the lawn. "I'm going to get my dog. Don't leave yet, Zeph. Wait here till I come back," he called over his shoulder and disappeared into the dark interior of the woods.

Ten minutes later Aaron came out of the trees, pushing a figure in front with Logan trotting behind.

"I think I've got our shooter. Found him up a tree," he shouted. Zeph met him halfway and clapped handcuffs on the dark figure.

When the three men entered the light streaming from the house, Catharine saw that the prisoner wore a devilish Halloween mask. She smelled the scent of a recently fired shotgun emanating from his bizarre black costume.

Zeph stepped up to the man, snarling, "Let's see what's under this vision of darkness."

He tore off the mask, and Catharine gasped as she gazed at the face of her husband's old tennis partner, Victor Hammond.

CHAPTER 40

After everyone left the crime area, Catharine called Marvina Brown, who was almost hysterical over her son's arrest. When she heard he hadn't done the shooting, she cried. "He's been having hallucinations, even with medication. He said he saw the devil in black."

"That was no hallucination," Catharine said. "They should bring Ralph home tonight. I'm sure the police will question him about why he was there. We still don't know the whole story. Can I come and talk to you tomorrow after he's home? I'll be able to answer some of your questions."

She choked out the word. "Please."

"I'll give you a call. Try to get some sleep. Everything will be all right."

Miriam Koster found a cleaning company with specialized equipment to get glass out of the furniture and carpet. Catharine cleared her desk. She surprised herself by her composure and lack of fear.

❦

On Monday Catharine drove to the Brown house alone. She had heard from Zeph about what happened. Now she wanted to hear it from Ralph. Parking in front this time, she noticed the mowed lawn and a few flowers planted in front of the sad-looking porch. Not even the morning sun could help the desolate-looking house.

Catharine knocked, and Marvina came to the door, looking as chubby as before in pants she had long outgrown. A too-large T-shirt topped her off, hiding her mountainous top like a tent.

Marvina threw her arms around her and said, "I've been waiting for you. So has Ralph, but he's not in good shape. He's still pretty shaken."

"I hope he doesn't blame me for what happened."

"He was too confused by the police to think. He kept saying the Devil wanted him to kill that nice lady."

They sat down to talk in the bare living room as before, and Marvina invited her son to join them. Ralph came in, his head down, not meeting her eyes.

"Tell Catharine what you told me," his mother said.

With coaxing, Ralph told his story in starts and stops.

"A man in black came in the store. He said he wanted to talk to me. He had on dark glasses, even though it was night out. He said no one else could see him, because he was from another realm. There wasn't anybody in the store anyhow, so what difference did it make? He said he'd pay me to do somethin', and he would come back. I was so scared.

"He came to our house, and Mom was at work. He looked like the Devil. He asked if we had a gun for protection. We had a shotgun, and I showed it to him. I don't remember much, 'cause I was so scared. He talked about monsters. He said they would leave me alone if I shot Catharine. If I didn't, the monsters would kill me. I believed him, and he gave me a black suit and drove me to your house and took me to the back and said to shoot through the window.

"I saw you and couldn't do it. You're nice. He got real mad and cursed. Then he took the gun and shot it. He said to run down the road till I got home. I did. I was scared. I ran and ran. Then the police came."

Catharine took up the story. "And the man in the Devil suit threw down your gun and ran into the woods, where he planned to escape in his car parked down the road. The police found it the next day and impounded it. He set you up to be blamed for the shooting. But instead he got caught by my husband's dog."

Marvina leaned forward, listening to Catharine, her eyes wide. "Who was the man?"

"He was an old friend of Kenji," she said. "He was trying to find and destroy research my husband had done at the Physics Institute, where they both worked. By getting rid of me or maybe just scaring me, he thought he could stop our investigation into their nefarious scheme. He may have gone after Aaron next."

She continued, "He was cleverly posing as Ralph's hallucination. Who would have believed Ralph?"

They sat in silence for several minutes, digesting what had been said.

"By the way, Marvina, I saw a lady who looked so much like you when Aaron and I had dinner in Harrisburg the other day."

Marvina chuckled. "I think you saw Shelly. She lives in Harrisburg, and she and her husband were celebrating their thirty-fifth wedding anniversary. She's my twin sister."

☙

"Do you think this is all finished, Aaron?" Catharine said later at the cleaned cottage, now fitted with a new window and screen.

"You don't, do you?" he said.

"No. Maybe Kenji did die of a heart attack. We can never

know because of the cremation. And Marti—what about Marti? It's too much of a coincidence. Miles, maybe. I want to research any drugs causing or mimicking a heart attack. Remember the incident in Switzerland a few years ago? I would need some medical expertise and someone to find out how Marti was disposed of."

❧

Sarah and her mother hadn't heard the news. On Tuesday Catharine saw her mother and sister; they both seemed content in each other's company. Catharine smiled inside.

Sarah called her aside to tell her something. She was almost euphoric. "I found the family documents you left in the big desk." She went to the desk and took out one of the papers. It was small, like a half sheet. It looked like Rachel's death certificate.

"Rachel's records?"

"Yes, it says here that Rachel died of a congenital heart condition."

"And?"

"Mama used to call it SIDS, and experts said it happens from the way a baby is lying in the crib. Well, I always thought I had caused Rachel's death because I picked her up the night she died after she had been put to bed. I was seven years old, and Mama said to never pick her up when she wasn't around. But I loved her so much. I picked her up to cuddle, kissed her good night, and laid her down again."

"Oh Sarah, you mean you've carried this burden all these years?"

"Yes, later I recognized it probably had nothing to do with me, yet I couldn't shake the possibility. Now I see it was something she was born with."

The two sisters hugged, and Catharine cried for Sarah's lost years away from her family.

Then she shared with Sarah a brief description of what had happened at the cottage on Sunday and about Kenji's missing research papers.

"There's a lot more I need to tell you, Sarah, about Kenji. Then you can counsel me about whether or not to tell Mama."

Sarah looked serious as she said, "Go ahead."

"To start with, Kenji was married at eighteen, but he never told me. The marriage was with a young Mennonite girl, and her parents annulled it and sent her away to distant relatives in Canada. Kenji didn't know he had another son until just before he died. This son is a doctor in Edmonton. I've told you the basics, and I'll answer any questions you may have, if I can."

Sarah sat stunned, then hugged Catharine. "We both have our soap operas, don't we?"

❦

On Wednesday Catharine received a conference call from Mae and Darian. After preliminary greetings, Mae said, "Darian and Gloria want to spend their vacation visiting you in August. Are you available?"

The request took her by surprise, but she said, "Of course. We would love to have them."

Darian said, "I want to know all about my father: where he came from in Japan, his family. And you said I have a half brother who's also a doctor."

"Oh, yes. It would be wonderful." Catharine bubbled over with joy. Tears ran down her face, tears of happiness for this new relationship. "In fact, I have a journal he wrote. I think you'll want to read it."

"And something else," he said. "I would like to help you look for those missing research papers."

"By the way, Gloria is expecting early next year. We'll want to get our visit in before then."

"Congratulations!" Catharine and Aaron said in unison.

"We'll be grandmothers," said Mae. "Me for the first time."

When she hung up the phone, Catharine felt elated. Mae had included her in the family.

✍

As Catharine and Aaron cuddled in bed that night, they discussed recent events. He was preparing to take a trip to a Christian university for three days to fulfill Dr. Kerry's requirement that he gain more knowledge on creationism before classes started in September.

"You know, what does it matter if we have proof or not? It would be great to find Kenji's research and see it published. Some would believe it, but many wouldn't, even if it was irrefutable. The plainest evidence couldn't convince them God created the world and they were wrong about life," he said.

"You're right, and maybe we will never find the research. "I hate clichés, but nothing says it better than God's people don't need proof, and His enemies wouldn't believe it anyway."

"I think we owe it to Kenji to locate those papers. I'm in it for the long haul, along with your new relatives."

"I knew you'd do it. You're adventurous." Catharine giggled.

"There are many unanswered questions like who visited my mother at Eden Court claiming to be a cousin. He doesn't meet the description of either Lager or Hammond. Is there someone else behind this?"

"But let's take a rest from thinking about the case for a while," he said.

He hugged and kissed her, but then she sat up suddenly.

She remembered the scene of the "glowing" ark of the covenant at the Mennonite Visitor's Center. *Could it have been a sign?*

"You know what? We never asked if Kenji went to church in Edmonton—he would never miss church. Maybe he gave the papers to someone there to hide. I'll bet it was the church with the Old Testament sanctuary model, and I think I know where he hid his research."

Aaron pulled a pillow over his head and said in a muffled voice, "Good night, Cat. We'll talk about it in the morning."

Printed in the United States
By Bookmasters